To Derek

From Mum

22nd Aug. 1993.

A Start in Life

Also by Ian Grimble:

The Harington Family, Cape (1957)
The Trial of Patrick Sellar, Routledge (1962/3)
Chief of Mackay, Routledge (1965)
Denmark, Routledge (1966)
The Future of the Highlands (co-editor and co-author), Routledge (1968)
Scottish Clans and Tartans, Hamlyn (1973-90)
Regency People, BBC (1972)
The Seawolf: The Life of Admiral Cochrane, Blond and Briggs (1978)
The World of Rob Donn, Edina Press (1979)
Clans and Chiefs, Blond and Briggs (1980)
Highland Man, Aberdeen University Press (1980)
Scottish Islands, BBC (1985)
Robert Burns, Hamlyn (1986)
Castles of Scotland, BBC (1987-8)

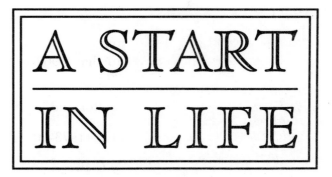

A START IN LIFE

Ian Grimble

The Book Guild Ltd.
Sussex, England

The Book Guild Ltd.
25 High Street,
Lewes, Sussex.

First published 1993
© Ian Grimble 1993
Set in Baskerville
Typesetting by QBF,
Salisbury, Wiltshire.
Printed in Great Britain by
Antony Rowe Ltd.,
Chippenham, Wiltshire.

A catalogue record for this book is
available from the British Library

ISBN 0 86332 831 8

1

The sea-birds watched, motionless, as the two boys wandered down the steepening grass slope until they reached the cliff and there paused. The larger boy (though their ages were the same) ran his eyes over the waters of the bay to its margin of white sand, then back again contentedly to the headland. Behind him white houses sheltered in its hollows, amongst little fields that mapped each scanty patch of soil. At his feet a zigzag track twisted to the cove below him. He started down it, calling to his companion:

'Mum was telling me, when she was at school, they came down here at dinner time. Isn't it a terrible long way to come, Donald, and back in an hour?'

Donald was still standing where the path began, gazing dreamily down, deep into the transparent water. He could just see the fronds of seaweed swaying with the tide against the rocks. Some shags were perched above, almost at the water's edge, and as they scanned the sea for prey their long dark necks swayed in a gentle unison with the seaweed. Donald himself swayed on his ledge above the track, lulled by this rhythm, until his friend's voice recalled him to action as it always did, and he scampered down the pebbly slope without any of his leader's sureness of foot.

He tried to imagine his own mother doing the same as a girl at school, which was difficult because she had never once mentioned going to a school. He resolved to ask her about that, while he slithered as he tried to get to the bottom as fast as Angus. It was an advantage in a way to be dressed in the kilt. But he was the only boy in the community who possessed one, and this had engendered a feeling of resentment against it which made him think the kilt made him slower. Once he had asked Angus why nobody else wore one and he said it cost such a lot.

The track was supported in the steepest places by dry-stone embankments, neat jobs of work that had survived the dilapidation since the cove had ceased to be used as a port. The path would double back beneath them, and already Angus had reached the bend below. Donald stood hesitant, looking down the loose scree, realizing that the only way to catch up with him was by a short-cut. Then he started nervously over the edge.

A sudden avalanche of stones made Angus turn, and if he had not happened to be directly in its path, it would probably have carried Donald slithering over the next embankment and thence to the bottom. Angus only had to catch him by the arm to stop him, which he did, laughing, as the pebbles clattered on the old wall below. Then he noticed the misery in Donald's expression and remarked casually, as though nothing had happened:

'To think Alec Fraser carried two sacks of meal on his back up yon in the old days.'

'That was a weight for him, Angy.' And as Donald stared back up the cliff, slowly brushing the dust out of the folds of his kilt, he thought, anyway old Alec never went up and down the path as he did with nothing on his back, just for the fun of it. Or perhaps he did, all the way from school at dinner time. Angus would know. Every spot was like that with Angus, a place where something had happened or someone had been. Whenever he imagined he had reached a secret place that was all his own he would find that Angus's folks were there before him, appearing from nowhere. He looked around, as though searching for some feature on which he could put a story of his own.

Angus had wandered down the shingle. It had been banked in concentric ridges by winter storms, and below the stones there was a narrow fringe of sand left dry by the ebb. Angus was a large boy for eight years and he moved with an assurance that was enhanced by his feeling of mastery in Donald's company. He exercised the same effortless influence over all the children of his own age in the district. But while it was asserted by intimidation to some extent in other cases, in Donald's it was based solely on affection. This was what he gave in return for the admiration that Donald was too young and artless to conceal. So to Donald he never showed himself as

6

one with a temper to beware of and uncertain impulses, but always as the source of adventure, the merry guide, teller of tales. It might be a fine thing to make other boys keep out of your road with a frown, just that, or maybe one of the words he had heard his elder brothers use, but it was not half so satisfying as to know that someone thought everything you did and said was right. Angus wriggled his gym-shoes in the sand by the ebb, and considered what they would do next.

The cove dug into a wide fault of rotten rock halfway along the right-handed headland of the deep bay, and its protecting arms reached round, but not far enough to give safety here from the fury of the northern seas. In earlier days a concrete jetty had been added to one of these promontories, which gave a last picturesque touch to the disused port on this placid August day. The jetty, and the old upturned boat resting beneath the stout wall at the foot of the zigzag path, were all that remained as memorials to Angus's forbears, who had gone north from this precarious anchorage to seek their livelihood. The place bore merely the functional name, The Port, and now it was not even that any more.

Donald was still standing by the up-turned boat, running his fingers over the tarred surface of the hulk as though he were a blind child trying to read Braille.

'Angy,' he called, 'isn't it a pity we can't take her out in the bay!'

'It is a pity right enough,' said Angus, and was still wondering what to do instead when Donald thought of a story for the boat. He had raised his eyes from the hulk to the soft, low island that lay out beyond the bay and suddenly he gave a little jump of excitement.

'Do you mind the boat was kept up the river last year?' he called with suppressed glee.

'So she was.'

'And Neil and the others rowed her out to the island and – and were trying to get her back to the curing station.' A story at the expense of Angus's elder brothers was the best of the lot, especially when it began with them telling him to run off and not get in the way. But Angus began to take over the story, unable to contain himself.

'They tried to row in against the tide,' he shrieked, clapping his hands.

7

'It must have been an awful strong current,' Donald put in quickly to keep the story his. 'They were rowing for hours and hardly moved an inch by the skerries.'

'Two hours it was anyway,' Angus chimed in, 'and wasn't Jackie red in the face?'

'But why didn't they come round here instead?' asked Donald to give his story the finishing touches.

'Because they left me behind. There was no one to tell them. You should have seen Neil's hands next day.' Angus collapsed on the shingle and threw pebbles quickly, one after another, into the water. A sandpiper that had alighted daintily on the glassy rim of the foreshore made off, skimming the water.

'We'll go out to the point along the rocks,' Angus decided.

'What about the tide?' asked Donald, hesitantly.

'It's a long way out now. We'll have time if we hurry.' And once again Angus led the way.

It was easy scrambling and hopping over the broad flat ledge of rock left uncovered by the low tide, though the surface was too jagged to manage without shoes. So when they had to wade, they sat down on a dry patch of rock beyond each ford, dried their feet on a grubby handkerchief, and put on their gym-shoes again. They passed many deep pools that delayed them while they gazed in wonder at the beautiful colours and sudden movements in these small, separate, living worlds. They trod upon twisted seams of marble, and skirted rusty-looking veins of ore. As they rounded the Port's right promontory the whole bay came into view, the dunes behind, and between their humps patches of field all mauve with scabious. They were approaching the colony of shags now, which clustered at the water's edge, their necks leaning and swaying, while one of their number wheeled off from time to time, rode the water for a few moments, bobbed down like an enormous float at the end of a line, and seemed to be lost forever. Only if you watched closely you noticed that really it had returned to the rock with the rest. Donald kept his eyes fixed on one in the water as though only his attention could save it from drowning. In doing so he got his shoes wet, which made him slip and graze his knee.

'It's all right,' he said as soon as he could see that Angus was really concerned. And on they went, skipping between pools and seaweed until they reached the point.

8

The headland ended in a sheer cliff of smooth dark rock. The two boys perched motionless beneath it were mere specks in these huge surroundings. Nobody on the opposite side of the bay would have noticed them there. Separated from them by about thirty feet of heaving water, an island as precipitous as the headland rose from the deep blue sea, its sides bleached by the droppings of innumerable birds, its summit crowned with matted grass. Fingal, the father of Ossian, had sundered it from the mainland with one blow of his sword, and it was called *An Caisteal*, The Castle.

'Will we see a gannet, do you think?' whispered Donald. The deep chasm of water between island and headland rose and fell like a monster of terrible strength breathing in its sleep. Donald listened to the throaty gurgle that echoed down the walls while he gazed at the delectable island opposite.

'I wish we could get across.' He was still whispering, afraid of waking the monster.

'Maybe we could do it in a boat,' Angus replied. 'They were climbing it for eggs once.' Donald's eyes swept over the bare, steep rock, searching for footholds. Suddenly a fulmer dived across his field of vision with incredible grace and speed. The boys watched it soar above the cliffs and hover there motionless on outstretched wings. They had been standing close to the water's edge, and while their eyes were aloft an exceptional swell washed over their feet, hustling them back to a higher rock. They laughed to one another over the mishap, until each caught the concern in the look of the other.

'We ought to get back,' Angus threw out carelessly.

'We were not here long.'

'Is that the truth?'

Although he tried not to hurry, Donald now found himself in the lead: and what was so sinister was that there was no seaweed on the route he chose, and hardly any pools. He looked for comfort at the little white houses scattered about the headland across the bay, far out of earshot. Where were the shags? Donald glanced over his shoulder, and saw that they had moved to the castle island. This was their world, not his. His thoughts flew to his own home, his secure haven where tea would be waiting for him. He began to feel hungry, though the sinking feeling in his stomach was not caused by hunger.

'We should never have gone to the point, Angus,' he said

breathlessly.

'Don't be silly. We should have brought a line and fished for cuddies while we were at it.' The remark brought back the old sense of fun and adventure for a few moments.

'I wonder who yon will be,' said Donald, pointing to a black figure that was moving across the distant sands of the bay. But curiosity died almost as soon as the words were out of his mouth. For they had reached one of the fords of the outward journey and it was no longer there. Instead there was a broad tongue of sea that licked exploringly up the creek until it reached vertical rock. Angus came to the edge behind Donald and looked.

'Maybe we could get across without our clothes, one of us anyway, and the other throw them over,' he suggested. But Donald was not to be comforted. He sat down and burst into tears. Just when life had seemed so idyllic, it had turned into a nightmare. What if he were to come home with his kilt soaked and late for tea, with the excuse that he had been cut off by the tide? He might never be allowed to his cove again. Over this sense of impending loss flooded the waves of his insecurity like the heaving sea up that creek, engulfing the school, the shop with its gossip and chocolates, the peat banks, the hay fields and the river, separating him from the living community across the water by ever-increasing tides. He longed to appeal to his mother but she was on the other side. When he tried to visualize her, he thought he saw her calmly discussing the crisis with some stranger. When he looked up, Angus was no longer beside him. He scrambled to his feet and gazed round him in a panic until he saw Angus away back under the cliffs, waving his arms.

'Come over here,' he called. 'We'll go up the cliff.' Donald stumbled over, rubbing his nose with the back of his hand, and looked up.

'Do you think we can get up there?' he asked dubiously.

To their right a broad seam of stratified rock slanted away to the highest point reached by the cliff along this headland, and then doubled back again like a huge imprisoned spring. On the other side of them the grass slope spread farther down, giving way to buttresses of sharp besalt, some of them leaning over to form gullet-like caves within their fangs. But between the huge spring segment and the torn rocks there was a gully down which patches of grass grew on tiny ledges, and the minute plants that thrive in salt spray. It would not have been hard for a grown man to make his way up this gully, but the spaces between ledges were wide for children of eight years. That was the worry, not its steepness. They were accustomed to heights and depths, and had often stood on the very edge of Fingal's precipice (from which visitors recoiled in horror) watching the screaming gulls circle against the heaving channel far below.

'I thought this was the best place,' said Angus. 'You go up first. You'll be better on the rocks than me.' So he gave Donald the incentive of leading while he was able to watch his progress from behind.

'I wouldn't start there, though,' he added, as Donald went straight to the nearest shelf of rock with desperate determination. 'It's not just handy further up.'

Donald was recovering his equilibrium under the calming influence of his friend. And in his desire to show Angus that this was so, he almost dawdled as he made a survey of the rock face. Then he began again in a different place, catching a ledge with his hands and heaving himself up. He wriggled round the protruding face and up the crack behind, until he stood on the first pinnacle. Next he had to get across a gap to the main face, which he did precipitately, toppling forward and catching at the ledge. He had not looked first for his foothold, but fortunately he found one after scrabbling with his feet a bit against the smooth surface. Instead of learning his lesson, however, he was lulled into supposing that he would always find a place for his foot by feeling about. The next time he thought he had discovered a ledge in this way it was only a plant growing out of a crack. The sensation of his feet slipping away just as he was relaxing his arms unnerved him, and for a second or two it was all Donald could do to keep his mouth shut and cling on.

Then suddenly his foot met something firm again, and soon he was able to swing himself up to the grass bank. Angus did not tell him that he had reached up to Donald's foot just in time with his hand. Soon the boys were up in the maze of transverse paths made by the rabbits, up over the slope dotted with blue and white gentian, on the ridge of the headland, exhausted and happy.

'Och, there was nothing to it,' breathed Angus, flinging

himself down and picking a full-petalled flower of Parnassus beside his elbow. He stared at the waxy whiteness of it and then said merrily to Donald,

'You're the great climber, Donald. We'll need to call that Donnie's Brae.' Donald rolled over on his face, repeating delightedly, 'Donnie's Brae, Donnie's Brae.' Then he jumped up.

'We'd best be getting home.' He could hardly wait to reach there to tell everyone the name they had given to the gully on the headland and why. They scampered down by the bay and took the short-cut through the sand dunes. Their wet gym shoes became clogged with sand, so they took them off by the roadside, sitting down beside the field of tall scabious and banging them together to shake off the sand. Then Angus went off to the left while Donald took the road to the right, over the hill to his home by the river. A weary contentment flowed through him. Old impressions of every summer he could remember passed through his mind in a jumble, until he came to the climb up the cliff. Then he fell to wondering how he would tell them at home about it, and trying to imagine the effect.

'Hullo Donnie, where have you been?' It was Christine, who lived quite near him.

'Only to the point,' he replied. Christine was younger than Donald. 'With Angus,' he added. He spun on his heels for a moment, aching to tell her how they were cut off by the tide. 'Well, cheerio,' was all he said, and passed on.

He could tell his father, just like that. His father would listen with interest: perhaps put in a question here and there. I wonder if that was the best way, he might say. But his mother was different. She might be fearfully upset: might even blame Angus. Donald decided not to say a word about it until he just happened to be talking to his father alone one time. I was cut off by the tide at the point that day, he would say in an off-hand way. So we climbed up the cliff. Angus is for calling the place Donnie's Brae.

Hugging his secret, Donald started to whistle as he pushed open the gate, and gave one or two shuffling kicks at the gravel as he went up the path. Through the window he could see them sitting in the study, the remains of tea spread out on a table behind them.

'You're a bit late,' said his father as he came in.

'I was down at the point with Angus. We got cut off by the tide.'

'For heaven's sake,' said his father, heaving himself out of his chair, 'you don't mean to tell me you were down on those rocks. However did you get there? And what have you done to your knee?'

'We went round from the Port,' replied Donald tremulously.

'Well, you're not to go down to the Port on your own again,' said his father angrily. Donald gave his mother a furtive, frightened glance, and found her eyes travelling over him.

'Don't worry the lad,' she said. 'Come here, Donald, and let me see your knee.' She touched the place where the blood had clotted, gently. 'It's only a graze.' She lent across to ring the bell on the wall beside the fireplace. 'Sit down and eat your tea now, then you can tell us all about it. You must have had a lovely time with Angus.'

Donald's father subsided petulantly into his great leather chair, while Donald sidled to one near the table and began to eat hungrily.

'What birds did you see?' asked his mother.

'Lots of them.' Donald's mouth was too full for more than this, but he swung a leg back and fore, and gave his mother a new kind of conspiratorial smile. She was on his side after all.

'We came up the cliff,' he confided to her presently. 'Angie is calling the place Donnie's Brae.' He chuckled. But once the first pangs of hunger were satisfied, Donald had time to notice something ominous in the atmosphere of the room. His father had made no comment on this last piece of information. He always had the last word and it had not come yet. Then the thunderbolt fell.

'Mummy and I have been talking about sending you away to school,' pronounced his father. 'We've found an excellent school for you, and we're going to take you there at the end of September.'

'But – but what about the school here?' Surely there could be no connection between going out to the point and being sent away from home. But if this was not retribution, what was it? 'I like the school here,' Donald added lamely.

'It's quite a good school,' said Donald's father, 'but we've found a better one for you in England.'

'In England,' echoed Donald helplessly. The word evoked no picture in his mind at first, then only an impression of green flatness and a maze of railway lines. The school map of England was almost entirely green, and the railway lines spread over it like a spider's web.

'Won't that be exciting,' his mother encouraged him.

'Will Angie and the others be coming too?'

'I'm afraid not,' said his father, 'but you'll be seeing them in the holidays.'

'Then why do I have to go? Is it because I went to the point?'

'Of course not. It's because it's better for you.' The tone was remorselessly final. There was a long pause, then Donald slipped from his chair and walked silently to the door.

'Where are you going Donnie?' his mother asked gently.

'Up to my room,' said Donald in a tone so flat there was not even resentment in it.

☆　　☆　　☆

Left to themselves, Donald's parents said not a word until Janet came in to remove the remains of the tea. She was one of the lucky ones, finding domestic service with the Hunters after she had left school, so that she did not need to leave home. After she had closed the door behind her, Mrs Hunter said:

'It was a great mistake to spring it on him like that.' Beneath the wide forehead her dark, slanting eyes looked out thought-fully, yet without focussing on anything, above high cheek-bones. The dreamy expression resembled Donald's.

'Nonsense,' snorted Captain Hunter. 'Donald isn't a baby any more. What he was up to today makes that clear enough. Wait till he has time to think about it. He'll be asking us how soon he's going every day for a fortnight before the day comes.' His wife ran a hand through her hair, already pure white, gazing at nothing. There was a long pause before she said:

'I thought he would be thrilled, especially as he's never been out of the Highlands. It was just so sudden.'

'That's not our fault,' said Captain Hunter. 'All that fuss about whether he was up to the right standard, just because he's at a village school. After all the delay, it was right to tell Donald as soon as we knew he'd been accepted. Not before.'

14

Mrs Hunter's hand still fluttered through her white hair, her eyes still focused on nothing in the empty fireplace.

'The strangest thing,' she reflected, 'is that he's never reacted to anything you said like that, before. If you asked him what's right, his reaction would be, what Daddy says.' She smiled slightly, enigmatically.

'And he'll soon realize I'm right again,' said Captain Hunter complacently. He leaned round out of the depths of his chair, raising his eyebrows with an expression of owl-like gravity.

'I'll tell you what the trouble was. He came back frightened by his experience at the point, or at any rate afraid of what I'd have to say about it. Anything would have upset him when he was in that state. You wait, my dear. He'll be as right as rain tomorrow.' Mrs Hunter continued to stare at the fireplace.

'But are you sure he should go so far away? You always spoke well of Glasgow High School, and you liked being there yourself. Couldn't he go to Glasgow a little later?' She spoke listlessly, as though going over old ground, and her habitual unsureness added to the hesitancy of her words.

'You know I've got nothing but good to say about Glasgow High School. But we've agreed that an English public school education is the best that money can buy, besides giving the boy enormous advantages in later life. Since we can afford it, we have no right to deny it to him.'

'But need he to go to an English preparatory school as well?' Facing defeat on the main issue, Mrs Hunter played for time, time for Donald among the surroundings in which he was so visibly happy, with the friends who evidently meant so much to him.

'My dear, we've been through all this dozens of times. If he's to go to a public school, he must start now. For one thing, he'll have to speak English properly.' Captain Hunter himself still retained the intonations of Ayrshire in his speech though he never used a Scots idiom. 'Anyway,' he went on, 'it's not for me to recommend an English education to you, my dear. You had one and I didn't.' It would have been hard for anyone except Mrs Hunter to tell whether this was intended as a complaint, a trump card, or a joke. And she appeared too distracted to consider such a question.

'Are you sure Donald couldn't go straight to Stellmore from here when the time comes, instead of going to a prep school when he's so young?' she pleaded. This time Captain Hunter played what was unmistakably a trump card.

'I know it's much harder for you than for me to lose Donald,' he said, 'especially when he's an only son. But we mustn't let our feelings interfere with his future.' Mrs Hunter gave him a swift, oblique glance and rose.

'I must go and change,' she said. 'The Joneses will be arriving soon.' With that she left the study while Captain Hunter flung himself back in his chair. He drummed on one of its leather arms with his fingers, though his expression was one of patient resignation. He had the sandy hair and slight, wiry physique that Donald had inherited, and a heavy way of breathing caused by the gas attack of 1918 that ended his military career. But the strongest feature was the determined cast of his eyes, and this chill purposefulness of expression furrowed his whole face as he sat there, planning to give his son the few advantages in life that had been denied to himself. He knew he was right, and was not much worried by his wife's doubts. She never could make up her mind about anything, and he was accustomed to doing it for her. Only he had to admit to himself that she could be disconcertingly definite at times, suddenly, unexpectedly. It was generally over something quite unimportant.

The sun was moving down the long sloping headland towards the sea. Captain Hunter became aware of the gigantic spectacle outside that was beginning to flood the study with such subtle lights. He heaved himself out of his chair with a grunt, and strolled out across the lawn. To the west the coast had been stripped of every landmark and indentation, and seemed to consist of nothing more than a few deft strokes of water-colour. and before these could dry, the sun was pouring pastel shades over the few defined outlines that remained, sinking sky and land and sea into a fantastic medley of crimson. Captain Hunter was suffused by a quiet satisfaction: and yet, perhaps alone of all the particles of this vast scene, the core of him remained apart, untouched. He turned to look up the river, dark and still within the shadow of the surrounding hills. All he could not see he imagined, the pools at each bend, the shallow water-courses, the very river-bed that he had explored so tirelessly, foot by foot.

Perhaps it was in these unfrequented places alone that he

found the cold complement to himself, in the rare moments of sudden tumult that stirred their mysterious depths. He stood, his eyes fixed on distance, and passed in review the many campaigns he had engaged in there. He dwelt on days of defeat and patient moments of victory, on the prizes lying along the banks. Disabled by his war injury, he had gradually narrowed the purposes of life to the pursuit of the lithe spring grilse, and its beauties to the grace of the midsummer salmon. He fell to wondering whether Bill Jones would renew his usual invitation to fish the broch pool on his stretch of the river, and glanced up the strath in search of an approaching car. He grew impatient, until it came into sight at last, gliding slowly over the bridge.

The whole family appeared to meet the Joneses. Standing at the sill of his bedroom above them, Donald leaned head and shoulders out of the window in expressionless anticipation. Mrs Hunter wandered through the door below him, a fur cape about her shoulders, her face troubled. She watched the Daimler creep closer, and her thoughts wandered to the tall white house from which it came, the crow-stepped gables, the corner turrets. But she did not picture it as the home of the Joneses. Her mind slipped easily out of the shackles of time, and she was imagining it in the days when it belonged to the old inhabitants, people to whom her own forbears were related.

Mrs Hunter looked up the settled strath, with its peaceful crofts and tidy holdings. Only one of the houses still had its thatched roof. Others had been replaced by corrugated iron, rusting and ugly. A few were slated. There were the ruins of other homesteads, gable ends still standing after a hundred years of neglect, tumbled walls. Mrs Hunter's imagination dwelt upon the malice of man that had eroded this little world without destroying it, the human capacity to survive. She could almost see the people who had been evicted from those river banks trailing down to the coast, digging the barren soil on rocky headlands, daring the sea from that crazy port where Donald had gone exploring, while the sheep farmers with their flocks moved into the lands they had left.

Again the cog lost its hold on the ratchet of her thoughts as she recalled that she was living in the former home of one of these sheep farmers, and William Jones in the very seat of the vanished Chiefs. A little smile crinkled the corners of her slanting eyes as she pictured the ebullient boss of the Jones and

17

Hunter Brewery in his role as a Highland patriarch. Her musings were cut short by a skid on the gravel as William Jones in person drove round the bend and brought his car to a halt.

'Hullo old boy,' he boomed as Captain Hunter turned to greet him. 'Having a look at the river? It's swarming with fish but I can't get them to nibble. Hullo, Katrine. Yes, you must come up one day next week and see whether you can do any better yourself.'

Hunter nodded. He never interrupted the flow of Jones's talk, particularly at the moment of meeting. It subsided in due course, and there were long respites when he was eating. You only had to avoid any subject with which he was not conversant: that would embark him on another that lasted until it was safely forgotten.

'I'm worried about the broch pool, though,' Jones continued. 'It's so accessible. I'm certain it's being poached, and what's more, I suspect that rascal Neil Magnus. He's one of the best gillies on the river all right, but that's because he knows it too well. I'll catch him, though. Oh yes, don't let me keep you out here. I've just been telling the water bailiffs to keep a look out for him. That's why we're a bit late.'

William Jones stood, rotund and voluble, in the crimson light. His booming voice died without echo in the vast stillness, and his very bulk was no more than a dot in the expanse of the river mouth. Yet they had become as much a part of these surroundings as that huge boulder beneath the sand dunes opposite, carried down the strath in a remote ice age and deposited there. Like the Hunters and Angus and his brother, Neil Magnus, William Jones had been deposited here by the forces of circumstance and he too belonged to this place.

Captain Hunter was trying to marshal him towards the door through which the ladies had disappeared already. When the men joined them in the sitting room, they found Mrs Hunter listening while Mrs Jones talked as continuously as her husband. She was imparting the gossip of last winter's season in London, clearing out her cupboards of memory to make room for the summer happenings in the Highlands with which she would regale her metropolitan acquaintance in due course. She was a sparrowy little woman of middle-age with a sharp nose and a gimlet expression of the eyes, and she spoke with a gushing self-confidence. This was scarcely surprising. In Lon-

18

don her audience consisted largely of people who would welcome a visit to the Highlands while up here she spoke exclusively to people who were, in varying degrees, dependent on her and her husband.

'Well, the Labour government has been in office two months and we haven't had our throats cut yet,' said Mrs Jones. 'Ramsay MacDonald is even said to be quite a courtier. But of course he's had time to learn.'

Mrs Hunter nodded sympathetically and made a non-committal sound without opening her lips.

'Give him a few more years,' went on Mrs Jones, 'and he'll be quite tamed. But I wish he would let someone help his daughter choose her clothes. My dear, she looks so rustic, which is all right in the country of course, but in London – well.' Mrs Jones completed her comment by fingering the large brooch of silver set with cairngorm stones and coloured pebbles, with which she had symbolized her own return to rusticity. There was affectation in the gesture, but none in the intense expression of her dark, pebbly eyes. Mrs Jones and her brooch also belonged to this place, even though she spent half the year wearing diamonds in London.

'Everyone's saying that Baldwin will soon be back, though,' boomed her husband jovially during the brooch-silence. 'The Liberals and Conservatives between them are sure to be able to dish the Socialists before they can do much harm.'

'I suppose that would be better for the Highlands,' said Mrs Hunter uncertainly., 'I mean, most Highland Members are Conservative or Liberal, and know more about country things.' She stopped, confused. A moment earlier they had all been in London on the wings of Mrs Jones's words. She was about to add that Socialists always seemed to be talking about city life, which would have sounded terribly rude to her guest.

'Shall we go in to dinner?' she suggested, and even now she sounded indecisive.

As soon as dinner was over, she slipped away from her guests. She always went to say good night to Donald at this time, and it was the time for confidences. Never had it been more important to retain that confidence, perhaps to recover it. She stopped in self-mistrust at his door, then taking a deep breath, she opened it. The room was empty.

In one corner a clockwork train lay on its side, and a big

19

book of black and white pictures was spread out on the table, still open at the page he had been painting with water-colours. It was held down by a corner of the paint box. Mrs Hunter went over to the untouched bed, ran her fingers over the sheets as though her sight alone was not to be trusted, then hurried down to where Janet was washing the dishes in the kitchen. Her instinctive self-control was returning.

'That was an excellent dinner you gave us tonight, Janet, thank you.'

'Oh it was nothing special. I was wondering had I put too much salt in the soup. It came out with a rush when I shook.' Janet was a large capable girl, though graceful too, and she had a merry face. Her home was only a few miles up the strath, but she lived with the Hunters during the week.

'No, the soup was fine. Did Donald come down for his supper?'

'He was the quiet one this evening, Mrs Hunter. He just came and sat in at the table and stared at his glass of milk. He wouldn't touch a thing and he hardly said a word. He wasn't like himself at all.'

'He was tired,' said Mrs Hunter. 'He was out at the point with Angus. What time did he come down?'

'A bittie before Mr and Mrs Jones came.'

'He didn't eat much tea either,' went on Mrs Hunter in a level voice. 'But I expect he'll be all right in the morning. Good night, Janet.'

She went round every room in the house, not expecting to find him. Then she returned to her own room and sat there, perfectly still. Nothing could have happened to Donald, she felt sure of it, as sure as she could feel about anything. He had simply gone out. It was a beautiful evening, even if it was getting past his bedtime, and there was no reason why he should not have gone out, even though he had never done it before. He was growing up. He might even want to talk things over with a friend. A wan expression flittered over her face when she thought of this, and of her hopes when she had gone up to his room.

The fatal course would be to go out in search of him. Yet that was precisely what his father would be most likely to do. There was only one alternative, to say nothing. It was her characteristic solution. She rose and rejoined her guests.

20

'Donald all right?' asked Captain Hunter. She had no need to reply, mercifully.

'Norman's just been telling us,' said Mrs Jones, 'that Donald wasn't too pleased to hear he would be going away to school in the autumn. Poor little chap. Of course he's bound to be upset at first. But you wait. He'll be clamouring to go back at the end of his first holidays.'

'I hope not,' said Mrs Hunter wryly. 'I've been trying to persuade Norman to leave him here a little longer. It seems hard to send him away so young.' She wished she could change the subject. It was wrong to discuss Donald after what had just happened, like betraying confidences behind someone's back. She had only said that in the faint hope that the Joneses would side with her, and she soon realized that even in this she was mistaken. What was Bill Jones saying?

'High time he went away to his preparatory school. How old is he? Eight? It's late already.'

'Why?' put in Mrs Hunter.

'Why? Because it's time he started on the public school curriculum. You know, cricket, and so on. It will do him no good to stay here learning how to cut peat and that sort of thing.' Mrs Hunter appeared about to speak, but he waved a hand to silence her. 'What's more important, he should start to learn the King's English, and start mixing with boys of his own class.'

Paradoxically Mrs Hunter, who was the only Highlander in this gathering, was also the only one who spoke the King's English. Perhaps the others thought they did, especially Mrs Jones, whose Home Counties' drawl only occasionally lapsed into the vowels of Liverpool which her husband used habitually.

'We don't think about class in the Highlands.' Mrs Hunter had said it before she could restrain herself. Anyway, she thought, and managed to restrain herself from saying it, it's only a matter of money nowadays, and even that's an improvement. Fortunately, Bill Jones went on booming away, apparently unoffended, until suddenly he turned on Mrs Hunter with the question:

'You didn't go to a village school, did you Katrine?'

'Me? No.' The question startled her all the more because her thoughts had been elsewhere. Anyway, what was the point of such a question? The Joneses must have known she didn't go to a village school. They found out everything like that about people. Yet Bill Jones had actually stopped talking, was waiting for an answer.

'My parents were rather old-fashioned. First we had governesses at home. In the end I was sent to a finishing school. But times have changed since then, and anyway Donald's a boy. I've often envied him, growing up as part of a community as I never did.' She threw the disconnected remarks together as they occurred to her, like someone inspecting a hand of cards until they come upon an ace. 'Of course you know Norman went to his village school,' she went on. 'And found it entirely satisfactory,' she concluded abruptly.

She had wanted to stop the talk on this subject, and by accident rather than design she had succeeded. The men switched instantly to the subject of fishing, the increase of salmon in the river, the attendant danger that local people would poach them.

'Did you see the case of the two Glasgow fellows who were caught using poison in the Oykell?' asked Jones. 'Wicked.'

It was indeed, and most of the local people would have agreed with him if he had cared to discuss the matter with them. But coming as he did from one of the poorer districts of Liverpool, he did not find it easy to unbend among the neighbours who doffed their caps to him as the Laird. And although his nature was generous and kindly, his attitude to them was influenced by his success as a self-made man. He could not easily distinguish between seasonal unemployment in the cycle of rural life and laziness. Worst of all, his genuine love for the Highlands was nourished by those dreadful novels about their inhabitants which have always been more popular than any which describe the reality.

So it was that Bill Jones could confuse outsiders who raided the salmon rivers of the Highlands with poison and dynamite with local people such as Neil Magnus. He now proceeded to do so at great length, engaging Captain Hunter as his ally while Mrs Hunter gave ear to the gossip of London once more.

Janet came in to have a last look at the lamps before going to bed. As she passed Mrs Hunter, the two women exchanged a glance which told each that the other knew the secret. I gave him away, thought Mrs Hunter. Janet must have gone upstairs to see what was the matter. Perhaps she's just been back again. Perhaps Donald's not back yet. She tried to listen, not to think about Donald. But every so often she glanced at the clock.

Half-past ten, eleven, eleven-fifteen. At last the Joneses were going. Mrs Hunter tried not to hurry back into the house, thought of all the casual valedictory remarks that might sound appropriate.

'Funny. I thought them both rather tedious this evening,' remarked her husband when they were gone. Mrs Hunter smiled faintly and trotted upstairs. She crept into Donald's room, and lent over his bed in the darkness. He was in it and he stirred.

'I was having such a wonderful dream,' he mumbled.

'Well, go to sleep and dream it again.'

'It's no use now. You've woken me up.' Donald peered over the sheets as his mother glided out of the room, a golden outline in the ray of light from the landing. He felt sorry for the way he had spoken, only the sorrow was not really a part of him any more.

2

For Donald that evening had indeed possessed the qualities that belong to dreams, timelessness, improbability, happiness bathed in the magic colours of sunset.

But not the first part of it. That was when he had returned from his supper in the kitchen with Janet. Janet was a grand person, though she could be annoying when you wanted to be left alone and she was all for a joke. Of course she was only trying to cheer him up, and it was his fault because he wouldn't tell her what was wrong. Usually he told her everything but this time it was too difficult.

He had just sat down to finish painting one of the branches of the trees in his picture book when his mother had come in. She was wearing a pale mauve dress like the field of scabious behind the bay, and her fur cape reminded him of the rabbit warrens where they had climbed the brae. Funny, because they never saw a rabbit. She had bent down to look at the picture, which annoyed him as it looked its worst when it was only half-finished. He had said,

'Were you at school, Mummy?'

'Not when I was your age.'

'But did you ever go to school?'

'Yes, I went later.'

'Where?' He had gone on staring at the painting, twirling the paint-brush between his fingers.

'In England. Look, I'll show you where it was on the map.' She had picked up the atlas but Donald took no notice.

'Was Daddy at school in England?'

'No. Daddy went to school at home like you. Then he was at a school in Glasgow.'

So that was it. He was to be sent away like his mother. She was at the bottom of it. He had looked out at the familiar view from his window, over the river mouth to the distant island that Angus's brothers had rowed to, then back at his half-finished painting. The colours were all harsh and unnatural. The silence was broken by footsteps on the gravel outside.

'That's Daddy,' said his mother. 'He must have seen the car coming. I'll go down now.'

Donald had put down his brush and gone to the window-sill. Below were his parents, quite apart from each other, looking up the river. What were they thinking? It was the first time in his short life when he became instinctively aware of the barriers between people, even husband, wife and child. He could not have expressed his sudden insight in words. He simply felt separate, withdrawn from them, as he observed them withdrawn from one another. It was as though something that bound them together had snapped. The big black Daimler came crunching up the drive and skidded to a halt.

Mr Jones was a strange person to watch, with his booming voice that had such a curious accent in it. He was hearty and fat. And there was Mrs Jones with her silly fluttering manner, though she brought him lovely presents like the paint box. Mr Jones was his godfather and he had no children of his own, and Donald knew he ought to feel grateful for all they gave him. Yet for some reason he resented their kindness. It was an encumbrance, a superfluity, not the kind of thing he wanted.

Neil Magnus, poaching. The bailiffs told to keep a look-out. Donald froze at what he heard, then backed stealthily from the window-ledge, as though he might be caught spying in the enemy camp. Suppose Neil was planning to go out tonight with his net, and fell into the trap. They would creep up on him unawares, great shadows all around just as he was landing the salmon. Donald's heart missed a beat. To think they were plotting this in his own home. Even his father was conspiring.

A thought struck him. He could warn Neil. He could slip out while they were at dinner, and if he ran part of the way he would be back in no time. Then they would know which side he was on, and Neil would be careful. Perhaps he wouldn't even go at all. Donald tiptoed out to the landing and listened. When he heard the enemy move into the dining-room he sidled down the stairs.

The house faced the river from a little way up the slope on its east side. The best thing to do would be to go up the hill

25

behind, by the back door. But that would mean explaining to Janet. Should he take her into his confidence? It would be great fun telling her and she would be terrifically impressed. Only she might say she would have to tell on him. Anyway, it would waste time. Donald crept out by the front door instead, and round the right side of the house, the opposite side from the dining-room.

He swung up between the grey-pink outcrops of worn rock. The ground was exceptionally dry, but springy. When it rained the water fairly tumbled down the slope, but it ran away quickly, having little soil to penetrate, and now it had not rained properly for weeks. Donald skipped up lightly.

Well, for goodness sake! Janet's favourite expression danced through Donald's mind. There, as he breasted the summit, was Angus wheeling a bicycle along the road that had just come into view below him. He shouted till Angus stopped and turned, then started to run down the hillside.

'What have you got that for?' he asked breathlessly when he reached him.

'I borrowed it from the Minister,' replied Angus. 'Neil is at the football so he asked me.'

Donald took hold of the handlebar. It was a shining new bike belonging to the Minister's son, who was away visiting a relative.

'Did he mind you asking for it, with tomorrow being the Sabbath?' he asked.

'He was worried at first. But Neil will not be going out till tomorrow night. So I said he would be sure and not go till after midnight.'

'So then the Minister said it would be all right?'

'It would not be the Sabbath any more.' Donald drew a breath of satisfaction that he had joined the conspiracy before making his contribution to it.

'There's Jones up at the house. I heard him say he was telling the baillies to look out for Neil on the river.'

'Did he say that? What else did he say?'

'Just that. He said, that rascal Neil Magnus.' Donald tried to copy the speech, but he did the boom better than the vowels. They both giggled till they had to stop the bike.

'Come and we'll tell Neil,' said Angus, pushing it ahead again. 'It will make him laugh anyway. But we'll need to wait until the football is over.'

They wandered down the road, wheeling the bicycle between them. It was rough and narrow, for all it was the main road along the north coast. It came over the crest where the manse stood, and wound its way through rocky ground draped with whins, and ledges of field in which the hay grew tall and dry, and a few patches of corn. It might be a good year for the corn though it was still too early to be sure. Along a steep bank above one of the cornfields you could still see the faint traces of ancient ploughing through the grass. Here they had used the hand plough in the days when they carried the soil on their backs, to make fields where there had only been rocks before.

At the bottom of the slope the road passed beneath the great cliff. On the other side of it the rich glebe fields where the scabious grew joined the sand dunes of the bay. At about the spot where Donald had parted, earlier that afternoon, Angus stopped to stare up the slanting cliff face, with its broken edges of flaking rock.

'Do you mind the frost early last fall, that brought the rocks down on the road?' he asked. 'Jackie was working on the roads then, and he said they were gey heavy to lift.' He was turning to move on when he paused again.

'When Jackie was at the stones here a car came up, and the driver stopped to ask him where he was. After Jack told him, didn't he look up and see Morag's cow on the top of the rocks. She must have wandered out.'

' "However did that animal get up there?" asks the man.

' "Och, there's a whole city up yonder," Jackie tells him. Jackie told Morag when he went to warn her about the cow, and she thinks she's been living in a city up there ever since.'

'Did the man believe what Jackie said, do you think?' asked Donald.

'I expect he just thought Jackie was daft. But he would still have to work out how Morag's cow climbed up the cliff.' They both laughed, then Donald thought of one himself.

'Once when Hugh Winnipeg was walking along here . . . .' He stopped. Hadn't he left out something important? It spoilt everything if you didn't get a story right.

'Hughie was just back from Canada at the time,' he explained.

'So he was,' prompted Angus.

27

'And while he was walking along here, a car stopped beside him, and they asked him how far it was to Dornoch. So when he had told them, they asked him had he ever been in Dornoch.

' "What would I want to go to Dornoch for?" says Hughie. "There's only the jail there, and I'm not wanting to visit that".'

'And what did they say to that one?' asked Angus although he knew.

'They said, "You haven't travelled far from home have you"?'

There were others strolling in their twos and threes to the football field beyond the bay. Those who came from Donald's side of the scattered township took the short cut across the sands, as the boys would have done, but for the bicycle. When they reached the headland beyond, that they had explored in the afternoon, they pushed it up the sandy grass slope between the dunes along the beach and the rocky heights to their right, with peaty lochans in their hollows. A hidden valley lay between these, made fertile by the combination of sand and peaty soil. As the boys came over the brow, its neat clusters of houses appeared, the peat stacks low beside them because the next winter's supply had not yet been brought home. People chatted in their doorways, which commanded the best view of the football field, sloping down to the reedy bog at the valley bottom.

Though the field was on the most even ground in the district, a rise in it almost concealed one end from the other. This undoubtedly affected a team's sense of unity, and made for those exhibitions of individual initiative that sometimes carried a back on one side through the goalmouth of the other. But perhaps the absence of team spirit was not due entirely to topography, except in so far as hills nourish the spirit of individuality.

When Angus and Donald arrived on the scene, this spirit was abroad amongst a number of children of their own age, who were kicking the ball wildly through the lower goalpost into the reeds.

'Shall we go down and score a goal or two?' suggested Donald.

'No, let's just wait. They'll begin in a minute.'

Angus threw himself down beside his bicycle, where Donald

joined him. It was more dignified, sitting there among the older people, than playing with the children. But the teams stood about in two groups without a sign of making a start, while the great scarlet sun slanted away over the island. The opposing team was at full strength, as it was bound to be, having come by bus. Not so the home team, whose eight members speculated profanely about the whereabouts of the missing three.

'What have you done with Hector?' one of them shouted at a pair of girls, comfortably settled beneath a large cairn and talking earnestly together. One of them laughed, the other pretended not to have heard.

'He'll be here when there's something to be here for,' called the one who had laughed. At that moment a spluttering motorbike brought Hector into view over the hillside and he was greeted by a derisive cheer.

'Now I've come, we can start,' he announced, leaping off his bike.

'What, with only nine of you?' called someone from the opposing team.

'Where's the referee?' asked Hector. 'With him it makes ten. We can win easy with ten.'

A pair of ordinary boots were found for the referee, the ball was retrieved once more from the reeds, the sun had one peep of the football match before it disappeared undersea, and the game continued in the long twilight.

It appeared at first as though Hector's assurance was justified. Neil at centre-half tapped the ball to Hector at centre-forward, who lunged down the hill with it to the enemy goal. But in his impetuosity he kicked it wide into the reeds.

'That marsh should be drained,' he pronounced during the delay while the children were retrieving the ball from among the reeds. This was not only a favourite observation among the local inhabitants, it was also set out from time to time in the reports of distant panels of experts, on grounds of amenity or ecology or both. But the privilege of distant administration is a costly one, and the charges for all the examinations and reports on the subject had already swallowed up a great deal more public money than the actual draining of the marsh would have entailed. A girl with muddy shins found the ball and kicked it back, not very accurately.

Next time, Neil decided against risking the fortunes of his side with the erratic Hector. Instead, he dribbled forwards cautiously himself, winning thereby the vociferous approval of the spectators.

'Don't pass it on,' shouted one.

'Keep it to yourself,' urged another. Neil's squat, powerful frame was hunched over the ball, and whenever he encountered an opponent both Neil and ball were round or through him as though inseparably attached to one another. At last the goal-keeper made a desperate sortie. Bang went the ball, hit the goalpost with a smack that set it wobbling, and landed among the children beyond.

'Good for Neil,' shouted Donald, hitting Angus on the back. A girl walked by them as the ball was kicked off again.

'What's in it?' she asked Angus in Gaelic. Even some of the young people still spoke it to one another on this side of the bay, though if Miss Cameron, the school teacher, caught them at it in the playground she gave them a skelping. Angus gave a quick glance at Donald and answered her in English.

'Neil scored a goal that nearly brought the post down.' She moved on to sit with the talkative group of girls beyond. None of them was watching the game, and after they had made room for the newcomer not one of them was even facing it.

They soon paid the penalty. Jack in goal had punted the ball and, whether by design or luck, it landed right in the midst of the gossipers. They rearranged themselves so that they could study the match more seriously, encouraged by advice to move to safer ground. They continued to watch until one of them mentioned the letter she had just received from her brother in New Zealand. After that they were soon in a huddle again, talking of an uncle in Canada and a cousin in Singapore, drawing the far places by invisible threads to this basin on the headland until Donald, overhearing them, imagined himself in the very centre of the earth.

Into the gathering dusk blew the whistle for half-time. A relief referee had appeared, and he possessed a watch.

'I ought to be getting back,' said Donald, startled by the shrill note.

'But you haven't told Neil about the water baillies,' Angus replied. 'I know. Come away home and we'll tell Dad about it.' He got up a little stiffly, and hauled the bicycle after him.

30

When Donald took a last look over his shoulder at the match, Neil was ramming his way forward to score his second goal.

Angus's home was higher up, inland from the football field. It consisted of some ten acres of ground, of which his family had been tenants since before the Crofters' Acts, and which they had worked since they were evicted from the strath, though in those days it had been divided into two holdings, each supporting a family. In the books these were still entered as separate crofts, but the higher and more barren of them had never yielded more than a desperate livelihood. Yet it was the house belonging to this croft that Angus's family now occupied, for it stood in a sheltered hollow which protected it from the strong winds that raced over the heights. It seemed to have crept for shelter there like an animal into its burrow. Chimney cowls twisted above the gable-ends, and at the front a porch of corrugated iron had been added, with a second door. It was painted the same russet colour as the window frames on either side and the little gable windows above. But these were now black shadows in the white-robed dwelling: all, that is, except the window downstairs at which a paraffin lamp hung, beneath the undrawn blind.

Donald and Angus clattered in through the back door, but Donald found himself alone on the threshold of the living room.

'Well well, Donnie, come away in,' said Angus' father, dropping the newspaper he was reading. 'Were you at the football?' He was sitting in his corner, in the worn, comfortable chair with rexine arm rests, his legs stretched out in front of the fire.

'Hullo, Magnus,' Donald replied. 'Neil scored two goals. He scored the second one just when we were leaving.'

'Did he now?' The round tanned face was placid, and over it the look of welcome was still spreading slowly. 'Angus was telling me you were down at the rocks today. You should take a line with you next time.'

Donald felt shy and looked at the matting, then into the smouldering fire. A hood of iron roofed it in, a flattened home-made funnel that drew the peat smoke away up the wide chimney. It was brightly polished with blacking, and the plastered recess of the fireplace was spotlessly white on either side of it. If the recess were only a little deeper, thought

Donald, you could sit right inside it on a cold night.

Angus's mother came in with another lamp, which she set on the table next the inside wall.

'Hullo Jean,' said Donald.

'I'm glad to see you, Donnie,' said Angus's mother. 'Sit in to the fire. It's getting cold now, though we've had a fine sunny day.'

'Aye, it was a grand day. Maybe we could be doing with some rain, though.'

'The crops would be the better for it,' said Magnus.

'And how are your father and mother keeping?' went on Jean. She sat down beside him on the couch under the window, her hands still in her lap, her quiet eyes turned on him, giving by this attitude of concern a freshness to the question she had asked him so many times.

'They're both fine, thanks,' Donald replied. He thought he ought to say more, but he couldn't think what. He gazed at the long brass drying rail that ran under the mantelshelf. It must be six feet long at least. Then his eye fell on the paper in the lap opposite him.

'Is there much news, Magnus?'

'Nothing much,' replied Angus's father, tossing the paper on the table beside him. 'The United Free is still talking of joining the Church of Scotland.' He gave Donald a questioning look and was reassured. Donald had often heard discussions as to whether the United Free should come in, even on the playground, and showed that he understood with a nod. What he didn't understand was something about taking a vote, but he was not going to admit this to Magnus.

'Will they agree to it, do you think?' he asked.

'I'm thinking they will.' The reply was slow, thoughtful. Donald always pictured Magnus as one of the patriarchs. he thought of him like this especially when the Minister read a passage from the Old Testament, not one of the frightening ones, but those that told of sorrow accepted without bitterness and good things with gratitude. Magnus was not really such a very old man, but Angus had been born to him and Jean long after their other children, Jack and Neil and the daughter married in Fort William. Magnus was only a little over sixty, but in the eyes of a boy of eight that is venerable enough.

It gave Donald great satisfaction to be able to call people so senior by their own names, rather than Mr This and Mrs That, as he had to do in his own home. That was more like saying Good Morning, never mind what the weather was like. He was savouring his privileged position here when Magnus favoured him with further thoughts on the union of the churches.

'Of course, they won't all come in, and then the funds will have to be divided, and that will be difficult.'

This was beyond Donald's comprehension, but the pause that followed was broken by Angus in the doorway.

'It's too dark to go on playing,' he announced. 'Jackie and Neil will be in soon.' He slumped down on a wooden chair at the far end of the room and drummed with his heels, hands in pockets. His mother rose and moved to the fire.

'You must be hungry, the two of you,' she said. 'I'll just give you a bite to eat before the others come in.'

Donald watched her arranging the peats so that they formed a glowing centre. Now he felt hungry. He looked on as the frying-pan was hung from its hook over the fire, and the kettle was balanced on the ledge beside it, and the enamel teapot placed in the front to warm.

'I know you like them fried best,' Jean told him, breaking an egg into the pan. 'Will you drink milk or tea?'

'I'd rather have tea.' Donald and Angus sat in at the table by the wall and began to butter their scones. They had eaten their eggs too by the time the footballers' steps sounded on the flagstones at the back.

'Hullo Donnie,' said Jack as the brothers appeared in the doorway. 'I saw you at the game.' He was taller than Neil, although he was only seventeen.

'Did you win?'

'We did not. I let three goals through in the second half. I could hardly see the ball coming by the finish.'

'Did you bring the bike, Angie?' asked Neil over Jack's shoulder.

'It's in the stedding. I said you would not go out till after midnight tomorrow.' That reminded Donald.

'I was wanting to warn you they've told the water baillies to look for you on the river, Neil.'

'Who told you that one?'

'Jones is at the house the night. I heard him say so.' Donald coloured, wondering for the first time whether they would

33

think it wrong for him to have repeated what he had heard. He looked furtively at Magnus the patriarch. Then he couldn't resist blurting out with a chuckle:

'He called you "that rascal Neil Magnus".' He got the accent much better this time. Neil capped it.

'Do you know what I heard him say to one of his crowd at the broch pool last week? "I don't know how anyone can stick a winter here, with no one but the natives to talk to".' They all laughed except Donald, who was held by a tremendous thought. Mr Jones must class him and his parents as natives, since they stayed here in the winter. But this led to another that wiped his satisfaction clean away.

'I have to leave myself,' he said in a small voice. 'They are sending me away to school.' Magnus scanned the unhappy little face.

'Why, that's splendid,' he said. 'That will be a great adventure for you. And think of all you will have to tell us when you come home.'

'Do you mean that, Magnus?' Magnus was talking like his father. Yet how could Magnus say anything that was not true, any more than his father?

'Of course, Donnie. Any other boy here would jump at the chance. Didn't the MP say when he was last here on his rounds that the road to prosperity is the road south? Man, you're lucky.' But Donald just stared at Magnus with large, sleepy, incredulous eyes.

'I must be going home,' he said. 'Thanks very much for my tea, Jean.'

'It was nothing,' she replied. 'Be sure and come again soon.'

'You'll be late if you walk it,' Neil warned. 'I'll run you over on the motor-bike.'

'Your egg will be cold if you go out, Neil. It's all right. I can run part of the way.'

'I'll take you to the top of the road anyway,' Neil insisted, and went to fetch his bike from the byre. Donald thought, they won't hear the engine at home from the top of the road. He said good night to the others, and went to join Neil at the back of the house.

'Just come in any time, Donnie,' called Jean from the doorstep.

'Are you all right?' asked Neil over his shoulder. Then they

34

were off.

Donald had never ridden on the back of a motor-bike before and he was still dressed in his kilt. While they bumped slowly along the track the novelty of the sensation enthralled him, but when Neil began to accelerate along the road he shivered. Just behind the crest from which the road wound past Donald's house to the river Neil brought the bike to a halt. It was all over in minutes.

'Thanks for telling me about the water baillies,' said Neil as Donald clambered down. 'I'll not get caught.' He gave him a conspiratorial wink, and noticed the pinched, unresponsive face in the surrounding darkness.

'Don't worry about going away, Donnie,' he said. 'You'll always belong here. Always.'

'Cheerio, Neil, and thanks.'

'Cheerio.' The engine gave a whir and Donald began to run home. He couldn't tell whether it was the cold that kept his legs going, or fright in case he had been found out, or something behind him that he was running away from. He had never thought whether the door was locked at night, but he had no need to. As he closed it carelessly behind him, it startled him with a loud click.

No sooner had his head reached the pillow than he was sleeping the deep, dreamless sleep of weary children. So that when his mother woke him, it was not really a dream that he remembered. It was the vivid farewell glimpse of what had seemed until now the solid reality, before it slipped away into the realm of dreams.

3

In the lives of everyone there are moments, a day or a week, that remain indelibly engraved on the memory. The events of years may flow together and fade while these remain isolated and vivid. Such was the day of Donald's visit to the point. Other days seemed just as important while he was living them, other adventures with Angus, visits to Magnus and Jean, times when the Joneses brought him exciting presents. But as the years passed all these people, even his own parents, became fixed as he remembered them that evening, almost as though they had all been portraits on a wall.

Of course the memory was not uppermost in his thoughts all the time. Sometimes it was gone altogether, at others bits of it would assemble, drawn together by a chance remark or something that caught the corner of his eye. But six years later something occurred that restored every detail.

It was the last day of his holidays after leaving his prep school, and the very next morning he would be setting off for his first term at Stellmore College. The circumstances were not the same as when he had been told for the first time that he would be sent to a boarding school in England. By now he was used to such comings and goings. Almost unconsciously, he had learnt to act one sort of part in one place, and revert to his other personality in the other. He was hardly aware that this even involved altering his speech. But as Donald walked over the hill where he had met Angus wheeling the bicycle that belonged to the Minister's son, he was filled with a sense of foreboding, as though he were re-enacting a part with an unhappy ending. He had spent the day visiting people to say goodbye, but it was not this that depressed him. The early months of homesickness at his prep school were among the memories that had grown faint with the passing of the years, and saying goodbye had become an easy routine. It was the image of Angus in his mind's eye, wheeling the bike along that stretch of road, that swept him suddenly back in time in a way that made him shiver.

As he walked beneath the rocks to the glebe by the shore the chatter about Morag's cow filled his ears, and about the jail at Dornoch and the bike that was not to be used until after midnight. He looked up the steep cliff, but there was no cow there. In the field below, the scabious had not begun to flower. Donald had never seen the field mauve behind the bay since that day. The places he passed still held the old stories, but no new ones. He pretended to himself that he was keeping his visit to Angus's home until last because it was the most important, but in his heart he was afraid. Magnus was ill. It was nearly a fortnight since Donald had been up there in the house with the twirling chimney-cowls, and then Magnus had just sat in his chair by the fire, his face drawn, a silent oracle. Now at last he had taken to his bed.

'How is he?' Donald asked Angus as he came into the kitchen.

'He had a better day,' Angus replied. He was still taller than Donald, and his natural assurance was increased by the fact that he would soon be leaving school to help support his family. Neil was away fishing now and sending money home. Jack was still working on the roads but he had got married, and repaired the house on the bottom croft for himself. So there were only Angus and his mother in the house with Magnus.

'And how are your father and mother keeping?' Jean asked, turning from the kettle she had just hung above the fire. Her eyes were tired and she fiddled with a cloth drying on the great brass rail beneath the mantelshelf, then moved an upright chair back a few inches. Finally, with an effort, she seated herself on the couch beneath the window, bolt upright, and waited with her characteristic air of attention for an answer.

How could Donald say that his father hadn't been so well, that his breathing had been giving him trouble again, and that they had called the doctor? By comparison it was nothing.

'Oh they're well enough, thank you, Jean,' he replied. 'Have you had the doctor in?'

'He was here,' said Angus. It must have been the same doctor, no question of that.

'What did he say?' And because Donald had seen him in his own home so recently, Angus's reply hit him all the harder.

'He said, "How much can you pay me, and what have you got to pay me with"?'

'Issht,' put in his mother. She half rose from the couch, then sat down again and crossed her hands with determination in her lap.

'So you're off to your new school tomorrow, Donnie. It doesn't seem any time since you first went away.' The remainder of that day came flooding back, Magnus sitting in that empty chair with the newspaper, the egg and scones, the ride on Neil's motor-bike. Clear as it all was, it seemed to Donald a lifetime away already.

'It seems just like yesterday,' he said.

'And you haven't changed at all,' Jean added.

'Oh I don't know. I mean, I hope not.' It was the first time Donald had found himself arrested in mid-stream, as he swam from one bank to the other. He was invaded by a vague doubt as to his real identity, or whether he possessed one at all. People who are processing themselves through life are rarely troubled by doubts as to their identity. But Donald was no longer processing himself. He was being processed as the sole heir to Jones and Hunter's Brewery, and although he was not yet aware that this was the accidental circumstance which governed his life, he did know by now that he was being carried along by a strong current and that he could not swim against it. He had tried to do it. And he knew he was no longer the same person since he had given up trying, whether Jean recognized it or not. Of course she must see it. She was merely recalling someone she remembered. Perhaps she was challenging him to become that person once more. But how could he, or anyone, become the same person as they were yesterday? Now he realized the grounds of his foreboding as he came to pay this visit.

A little figure went by the window and came in at the door. It was Nurse Barbara. She looked all of her eighty years by now, and she sat straight down on the couch beside Jean, flustered by her walk up the hill. Her hair that she used to gather so neatly behind her head was now scattered in straight grey strands down her neck. She laid a tiny hand in Jean's and took a few gusty breaths.

'How are all my bairns?' she asked, and it was a fair enough question. She had brought Jean herself and all her children into the world. Not Magnus. It was just sixty years since Nurse Barbara had started work as the district nurse, and he was older than that. She had not delivered Donald either, whose mother had gone down to Inverness where he was born. But Nurse Barbara had become hazy about such things. For fifty years, until body and mind had weakened ten years ago, she had attended every birth in the district and nursed almost every sickness. She had trudged for miles in all weathers to stay in the house where she was needed, cooking the food, washing the children and the clothes. Her reward was to believe that everyone here was her child, that everyone owed their life to her. She had processed herself without marrying or giving birth into the grandmother of the entire community.

Donald was too young to have seen her stepping out on a six or seven mile errand through the snow. She still occupied the little house by the broch pool a couple of miles up the strath from his own. But he remembered her only since her retirement, the tall, slight figure bent against the slope as she passed his gate on her way to the village. But she had always treated him as one of her bairns, and before her mind became clouded she used to know as much about him as he knew about himself.

'We're all well here except Magnus, my dear,' said Jean. 'He's in bed yonder.' She pointed to the closed door of the little closet behind the stairs. Generally the two women spoke to one another in Gaelic, but they did not do so in front of Donald.

'Oh Magnus, yes, the poor soul. I was forgetting why it was I came,' Nurse Barbara replied, looking intently at Jean, the little hand still in her's. 'I will stay with you until he is better.'

'But Barbara, I would never let you do that. You have done us enough kindness in this house. We'll manage fine, thank you.'

'It will be no trouble, Jean, no trouble at all.' Nurse Barbara looked away into the fire with the kettle simmering above it.

'I was always wanting to be a nurse,' she reflected dreamily. 'I think when Magnus is well again I will go down to Edinburgh and see if they will take me for a nurse.'

Donald stood up and walked to the back door. There he asked Angus in a low voice whether he could see Magnus.

'He was sleeping just now. Wait till you come again and he is better.'

'Tell him I will be thinking of him,' said Donald, and with that he said goodbye hurriedly to Angus and his mother and Nurse Barbara, and left.

He felt deeply troubled as he walked past the outcrops of rock in the slowly fading light, down the brae to the short cut along the sands. He imagined Magnus, lying patiently in the little closet, and pictured Nurse Barbara with the tiny hands and wandering mind. Above, the stars were beginning to shine and in the distance, because the tide was out, the waves sighed rhythmically on the shore. The sense of impending loss that had begun to invade him on his outward journey, sweeping him back to that day of the football match, almost over-whelmed him in the gathering gloom. Nurse Barbara was changed altogether. Magnus would never again be the person he knew. Even Angus was no longer the merry companion of his youth, but serious and withdrawn, an adult almost. Per-haps Angus could not recognize him as the same person any more.

And how would he recognize himself? He turned to where the Port was by now hardly discernible on the headland beyond the bay, and the point where he had stood with Angus opposite the castle island. He could almost believe he saw himself still, perched on that rock, but when he looked back at the sands he saw that he was no more than the maker of footprints in them that the incoming tide would obliterate.

'You haven't changed at all,' Jean had said, and little could she have foreseen the morbid train of thought that her well-meaning words engendered.

Donald was very silent the next morning as his parents drove him to catch his train. He gazed from his window at the fawn hillside that stretched away to the skyline, and across to the other side where the strange-shaped lochans lay.

'Has that lochan got a name?' It was separate from the rest, near the road. It was almost oval in shape and inky black.

'It's called Loch mo Naire,' Mrs Hunter told him. 'That means Loch of my Shame.'

'I wonder why.'

'Anybody who behaved foolishly was dipped in it. The water was supposed to have virtue in it that made people wiser.' When Donald said nothing further, she added, 'I suppose anyone who had been thrown in there once at least had enough sense to avoid a second wetting.'

Nurse Barbara? Would they have dipped her? Of course it wouldn't have cured her, except that it would probably have killed her, and that might be called a cruel kind of cure. As though his father had read his thoughts, Captain Hunter said:

'It's appalling to think what went on in these parts before there were doctors around.' The doctor had visited him, and now he was fit enough to drive the car. He had visited Magnus, yet he was still lying, almost certainly, in that little closet. Perhaps the doctor had deliberately done nothing for Magnus, or perhaps he was like Loch mo Naire and couldn't cure everybody. There was another pool somewhere, Donald had never been told exactly where, into which people used to throw their precious coins in the old days in the hope of having their wishes granted. Donald thought of it as he recalled what had happened when the doctor went to the home of Magnus.

This was the first time Donald's parents had taken him to the nearest station, thirty miles away from their home, and left him there with his black trunk and wooden tuck-box to continue the journey without them. He said goodbye to them in an independent, matter-of-fact way and never looked round to wave to them from his corner of the carriage as the train pulled out. Mrs Hunter caught her breath as she turned away. She drew what comfort she could from the fact that Donald would be meeting his aunt in Inverness and travelling to England in her company.

'I do hope he's going to enjoy his first term at Stellmore,' she thought aloud as they began their journey home.

'He enjoyed his prep school well enough once he got used to it,' replied Captain Hunter confidently. 'And remember how you worried about that.' It had been his idea to send Donald to Stellmore in May, instead of waiting until the beginning of the new school year in the autumn. He repeated his reason for this.

'He's probably the only new boy in his house this term. That may make it a bit harder for a start, but he'll have a great advantage over all the other new boys who arrive next term.' Mrs Hunter considered this for a while, though she had heard it before.

'I do hope he will be happy there,' she said at length. 'He was so silent, so withdrawn.'

41

'He has more assurance, that's all, more poise. That's one of the excellent qualities you learn at these schools.' He glanced from the road ahead to his wife, realizing this was not quite the most appropriate observation for him to have made to her.

'I wonder whether that sort of self-sufficiency really is a good quality,' she reflected. 'I mean, I wonder whether Donald will be any happier if he becomes all self-contained, as happy as when he entered more into other people's lives.'

'You've got to remember that Donald's nearly fourteen. Adolescence is a difficult time for a boy.' Oh why must Norman always adopt the attitude that she couldn't be expected to understand? She went on thinking aloud, though now she was really talking to herself.

'When someone's character changes,' she mused, 'I wonder whether it's the gradual influence of months or years, or whether this can only be the foundation for something that happens suddenly. For instance, did Saint Paul's character really change suddenly on the road to Damascus, or did his vision set the seal on a change that had been going on inside him for longer than even he realized?'

This was not the kind of speculation that appealed to Captain Hunter, and whenever he felt that his wife was trying to undermine his confidence with her perpetual doubts it made him impatient.

'I don't know why you're fussing like this,' he said with the note of finality that he adopted for bringing such discussions to an end. 'Donald is developing like any normal boy.'

As he trundled south in his corner of the railway carriage, his parents re-entered the strath with its winding river. Captain Hunter's eyes darted towards it as often as he dared take them from the narrow, serpentine road, and when the car stopped at their door he leapt out with unusual energy. But his wife remained seated where she was for a while, unnoticing.

Towards half-term Donald received a letter from his father telling him that Angus's father Magnus Mackay had died. He added that Nurse Barbara had been taken away to a home. She had been unwilling to go, but she was unfit to look after herself, and she refused to live with anyone else in the district

42

for fear of being a nuisance. So it was right that she should be taken away, Captain Hunter assured his son, though Donald could not remember such a thing ever happening before. Even people certified as mentally defective were cared for at home by their relatives.

Donald pictured the procession of mourners winding down from the house in the shelter of the hillside, between the outcrops of rock, down the brae to the churchyard by the shore. His father hadn't told him whether Nurse Barbara had stayed in that house until Magnus died, or whether she had been put away before. He tried to imagine her, lonely among strangers in her hospital, away from all the people she had brought into the world and kept living in it. Or perhaps she was past knowing that the folk around her were strangers. Then he thought of Magnus, laid in the cemetery before the scabious had begun to bloom in the glebe fields. It was the first time death had taken anyone who was important to him, and his feeling of loneliness increased.

He had been finding it hard to learn the rules of life at Stellmore, on which he was to be examined at half-term. He had already failed a test on his House's sporting trophies, silver cups of all shapes and sizes that were displayed in a glass case in the dining-room behind the high table at which the prefects sat. But he hoped he had now mastered the rules of dress.

On weekdays boys in their first year wore Eton collars over the lapels of their blue suits, while those in their second year graduated to smaller starched collars with rounded ends. On Sundays the whole school dressed in tail coats with striped trousers, and silk top hats out of doors. You could not wear an Eton collar with tails. Both first and second year boys wore starched collars with rounded ends on a Sunday, so that there was no longer any way of distinguishing them by their dress. You could safely recognize a boy of over two years' standing on any day of the week, because he wore the same kind of starched collar with a pointed end, whether with blue suit or Sunday tails. Prefects, and also those who had won their school colours in any sport, enjoyed the ultimate honour of an unstarched collar. Prefects also carried umbrellas. So there were areas of ambiguity, as well as guidelines, over the status of the other boys. And this was extremely important, because of the rules about whom you were and were not permitted to talk to.

43

By chance, Captain Hunter's letter had brought Donald its distressing news on a Saturday. Sunday presented him with more immediate problems. In addition to the impossibility of distinguishing boys in their first and second years on that day, there was the ambivalence of the silk top hat. With the weekday uniform a straw hat was worn that had round it a ribbon of its wearer's House colours. Donald had learned by now who were the fifty or so boys in his own House. The difficulty was to recognize to which of the other ten Houses the remaining boys belonged and this, as he was to learn, was a matter of paramount importance. All you could tell about a silk top hat was whether it had been floated down the river, because it was never quite the same afterwards.

On this Sunday he dressed himself with more care than usual in the regalia of the English public school tradition, and prepared for the ritual of a divinity lesson followed by a religious service, an afternoon walk, and the evening service at which there would be a sermon. He feared the afternoon walk above everything, because he had discovered it to be the weekly test of his knowledge of the symbols, on the day when some of them were missing. He had observed how umbrella strode forth with umbrella, pointed collar with pointed collar. Condescensions on the part of a soft collar had not escaped his notice, and he had even spotted new boys and one-year-olds, as they were called, taking advantage of the absence of Eton collars. They would go for walks together at the end of a week during which not a word had passed between them. But one thing was taboo. No one must take advantage of the absence of straw hats with their House colour ribbons to consort with a boy in another House. Only the prefects were exempt from this rule, their privileged status being symbolized by black ribbons in their straw hats rather than House colours, as well as their Sunday umbrellas.

Hence Donald's weekly anxiety over the Sunday walk. It was a subtle test in one of the most important lessons taught by his school, one that was designed to impart a sense of the social distinctions. Of all the English virtues that Donald had come to Stellmore to learn, it was the most foreign to his native background. So he depended on symbols for guidance more than most of the other boys did, and on a Sunday some of these were withdrawn. It was as though they were being encouraged, once they had been told the rules, to develop a natural instinct of their own in this important department of life.

Donald had been left in no doubt as to its importance, and had done his best to study the rules. His desk stood in a study round whose walls ten other desks stood cheek by jowl, those of the juniors nearest the door, those of the most senior by the fireplace. In the centre was the table of the House prefect, which it was Donald's duty, as the most junior, to tidy and to dust. Consequently he knew that at one end of the room sat his seniors, with intermediate grades between him and them, and beyond him only the door.

On his first Sunday he had not left the school grounds, but on the second he had been bold enough to call across a vacant desk to the boy beyond, 'Shall we go for a walk to the river?'

This was not mere heedlessness on his part. He knew he was forbidden so much as to set foot the other end of the study, except to tidy the prefect's table. But Hobson's was well his side of the imaginary boundary, and Hobson was in a lower form than himself, and wore the same rounded collar on a Sunday as he did. It so happened that Hobson was doing so for his last term. The fact that Donald was in a higher form counted for nothing. Brains did not form a basis for status at Stellmore.

'You ought to know by now the river's out of bounds,' Hobson replied severely, and Donald could tell he was not simply imparting useful information but rebuking an affront to his dignity. He fell into a cautious silence. And for many Sundays afterwards he watched the member of an under-sixteen eleven turning down invitations for a Sunday walk because he had promised it to another, and studied the more successful pairings that offered a key to conformity. Once or twice new boys of the previous term strolled with him out beyond the bypass and by the track that led round by the water tower. But he always waited to be asked, and if nobody asked him he went by himself. He had grown accustomed to spending this break from the busy curriculum on his own by the time he received his father's letter, telling him Magnus was dead.

If only Angus were here, he thought. But it was six years since they had met at school every day, and Donald was forgetting how little he had seen of Angus in the interval.

After breakfast on this Sunday morning Donald sat down at

his desk, and so as not to be seen doing nothing he took out a glossy illustrated guide that his mother had gone to the trouble of obtaining and sending to him. He did not want anyone to talk to him, so he turned over the pages busily until he reached a picture that arrested him. It showed the local river, much wider than the one at home, sluggish by comparison, luxuriant with carpeted banks and overhanging trees.

'We'll go down and climb that tree,' he could hear Angus saying, unaware that the voice in his memory was that of a boy of eight. 'Then we could bathe.'

He smiled, thinking of the fun they could have if Angus were here. Never mind if the river was out of bounds. You would never get caught with Angus. He would be as sharp as Neil with the river baillies. Donald turned over the pages until he came to a picture of the oak tree in which Owen Glendower was said to have climbed. The description underneath reminded him of the heroes of his bedtime stories. He tried to imagine Glendower leading his men, not over snow-capped moor and through racing torrents but stealthily, by the placid river. Or perhaps he would only descend rarely from the Welsh hills on the horizon. How Donald wished these were not so far away.

He stared out of the window, dreaming that he might fly through it. The sky was almost cloudless behind the fretwork of transparent leaves. It would be cool and sun-drenched down by the river and there he could think about this thing that had happened, undisturbed. Donald looked round his crowded study, but his spirit had taken flight already, so that he scarcely heard the loud chatter. No more did he attend to the Head Master in chapel expounding the first Book of Kings, nor the bleating of the padre there.

He returned to lunch in his house and filed out of the dining hall with its display of silver trophies, last of all. He skidded down the passage to collect his top hat from his desk, where he picked up the guide book at the same time. Then he sauntered out of his House in as leisurely a way as he could contrive, into the sunshine.

'Fa-a-g.' The awful word came booming through the stillness just as he passed the crucial corner. When a House prefect called 'Fag' every boy of less than two years' standing had to rush to where he stood and queue up beside him. The last to arrive was at his command. But once outside the gates, you were safe. Just in time. It only took Donald a quarter of an hour to reach the bypass and, crossing it, to strike into open country.

Stellmore College had itself moved into what was then open country a century earlier, out of its cramped and ancient buildings in the nearby county town. But it had been planted within walking distance of this rural metropolis because it had been founded in the first place as a day school for its townspeople, like so many of the grammar schools established during the Reformation. And although it had evolved more recently as a boarding school for boys from other parts of the country, it had not been able to rid itself of the original responsibilities of its endowment. During Victorian times the school authorities had attempted to discourage local day boys by denying them a proper education, and for a while they had even been obliged to act as servants to the boarders. But when Gladstone became Prime Minister he instituted an enquiry that put a stop to this scandal.

'When I say the Lord's Prayer,' a gentle Dean and notable educationist of the time had remarked, 'I use the old form, and say "deliver us from the evil one." And I mean Mr Gladstone.' The consequence was that Stellmore had not been delivered from its local day-boys. And now that it was engulfed once more in the suburbs of the expanding town, it was as convenient as ever for them to attend the school. There were about fifty of them, formed into their own House with its House colours. Any unnecessary contact between them and the boys in the other houses was discouraged among the boarders.

When Donald had climbed over the stile beyond the bypass he removed his top hat, though he looked over his shoulder for strolling prefects as he did so. Then he started whistling at the sight of the long low hills of Wales in the distance. His parents had promised to visit him one half-term, and perhaps they would drive him there. Or perhaps they wouldn't bring the car such a long way. It was a terrible thought. They might just sit in one of the hotels in the town, or go for a walk like this. How could he tell them not to bother to come unless they brought the car? Though it would be fine to see them anyway.

If only they were coming next weekend for Speech Day he could ask them whether Nurse Barbara had stayed to look after

47

Magnus, and whether his mother had gone to visit Jean after his death, and things like that. He had mentioned the date of Speech Day in a letter, and his mother had written to ask whether he wanted them to come very much. He had replied that it didn't matter, and then his father had said in yesterday's letter that it was too far. He wasn't absolutely sure that he wanted them, car or no car. But then, he wasn't sure either whether they ought to come because everyone's parents did, and there was nobody he dared ask.

He stopped and looked at his guide book. A diagram said that to reach the river he ought to turn right, leave two farms on his left, and skirt a wood. He turned over the page to take another glance at the picture of it, but happened on the photograph of Glendower's oak instead. It was in the wood. Donald shut the book and followed the hawthorn hedge to its end, stepping out briskly. Was the oak one of innumerable trees, or would it be standing all by itself like the one at the edge of the hawthorn hedge? It must be very old. So perhaps it would be hollow, with great gaunt arms and hardly any foliage. You couldn't really tell from the picture. He thought of the Ancient Mariner, and this brought Magnus back to his mind, and he wished he could see him clear of these other images.

Most of the fields were pasture, though some of them had been ploughed and were lying fallow. The corn was almost full-grown already in others. All of them were enormous, even compared with the largest holdings in the strath. They rose and fell over the undulating landscape, intersected by rough roads, and dotted with spinnies and copses. The farm houses were larger than Donald's own home, with far-flung steddings, almost as large as the Jones's house. At the second one he passed, he stopped to stare at the ruminating cattle. They were pure Ayrshires, much sleeker than the cows at home which had tousled coats because they had been crossed with the Highland strain.

Perhaps he was unobservant, or possibly Glendower's oak was hardly distinguishable from the many venerable oaks in the wood. Donald was so eager to reach the river that he did not linger long, searching for it. Although he did not do it consciously, he was veering to the right where the ground fell with gathering steepness, and oak and beech gave way to hazel clumps. When the first shimmer of water glanced through tangled branches, he forgot Glendower's oak altogether, as he scrambled down to sit among the great roots which clutched the river bank like the fingers of a gnarled hand. And he gazed into the sluggish water.

His thoughts, so easily carried away into nothingness down imaginary rivers, soon slipped ahead of this slow-moving current. But now the eddy below him where the twigs and floating leaves revolved was the eddy of the broch pool, and behind him up the bank stood Nurse Barbara's house. Once Janet's parents had persuaded her to leave it and go to live with them. They had nailed up the door, hoping she would never want to return to her lonely dwelling. But one day Nurse Barbara had slipped away and climbed back through a window. She was not strong enough to undo the door, so she had gone in and out through the window until someone came to take the nails out. What had become of that house now?

'Hullo.' Donald jerked his head round and there, where Nurse Barbara's house should have been, a boy was strolling towards him. He was about the same height as Donald, though stouter, and he was swinging his top hat in his hand.

'You're out of bounds,' said Donald.

'Only because my parents aren't with me,' replied the other with a grin.

'Have they come to see you?'

'Oh no. You see, I'm a day-boy. I live up beyond the wood there.' He spoke deprecatingly, nodding his head over his shoulder.

Donald stared at him, fascinated. There were two day-boys in his form, but he had never actually spoken to one before. He had sometimes wondered what they felt like, going back home while he returned to his House with its web of taboos. But he was wary.

'How long have you been here, I mean at Stellmore?' he explored.

'Just over a year,' the boy answered, and he sat down beside Donald on one of the great roots.

'This is my first term,' Donald informed him quickly, but he did not get up again.

'What House are you in?' he merely asked. Donald told him.

'Rotten luck. I suppose your old man was there or something.'

'My Dad never went to a public school.' There was a faint jocularity in the way Donald tossed it out. He was beginning to lose his caution.

'I say, I wouldn't go around telling people that,' said the day-boy.

'Why?' Donald tossed a twig into the water and watched it sail down to the eddy, where it went round and round.

'Oh, I don't know. I wouldn't, though. By the way, what's your name?'

'Hunter.' Donald laughed as he said it. 'We don't use surnames much at home, and when I came to my prep school in England and people asked me my name, I said Donald. But everyone has different surnames down here.'

'Where do you come from then?'

'Oh a place in the north of Scotland.'

'You don't sound like it.' The day-boy was an open, jovial sort of person, without the same reserve as so many of the other boys.

'What's your name?' Donald asked him.

'Stretton.'

'And you live in that great farm?'

'It's only a hundred acres.' Pleasantly he changed the subject. 'Do you mean that everyone where you lived is called Hunter?'

'Oh no.' Donald laughed again. 'We're really foreigners there. My father's from Ayrshire. But my mother's family are from the Highlands and I was born there, so I sort of half belong.'

Stretton seemed puzzled by this explanation, and now it was he who stared at the twig revolving in the eddy.

'Anyway, what's the matter with my House?' Donald challenged him.

'It's the pot-hunting House,' replied Stretton, 'and no one thinks anything of you there unless you're good at games. But perhaps you like that.'

'We have fifteen silver jerries in the dining-room,' Donald confirmed. 'I see them whenever I eat. And last week I had a test on what they were for, and I got two of them wrong. I was told I was not keen enough on the House, and I was made to copy out pages of Pope's *Odyssey*.' But the worries of everyday

50

life seemed miles away from this world of sun and drifting water and companionship. 'Never mind,' said Stretton. 'You'll lose the under sixteen cricket pot this term, and then there'll be one fewer to remember. I say, you aren't a cricketer yourself, are you?'

The need for caution, never quite asleep, awoke in Donald again. He glanced at Stretton, and was reassured by his grin.

'All I can say is, thank heavens there's nowhere smooth enough for a cricket pitch at home.' Donald had never been able to talk like this since he came to Stellmore, and the sensation was exhilarating, especially when he was out of bounds by the river and also in the company of a day-boy. He was eating the forbidden fruit and it tasted delicious.

'Tell me,' he asked with happy abandon, 'is cricket really compulsory at Stellmore till the day you leave? When I think of the number of months I'll have spent by then, standing about doing nothing in white flannels, it nearly drives me mad.' Donald tore a tuft of grass from the bank, simulating madness.

'I can put up with the playing,' Stretton conceded. 'What gets me down is wasting an entire half-holiday watching the school match. Watching House matches is bad enough.'

'I suppose you'd rather be swimming,' said Donald looking dreamily into the water. 'Do you fish?'

'In the holidays mostly, but I caught a pike the other day.'

'Do you fish for salmon here?'

'Only between February and April.'

'The forbidden river,' Donald murmured, staring into the quiet reflections.

'Why do you say that?' Stretton asked quickly, struck by such an odd remark.

'Well, it's a funny thing about rivers. They always seem to be out of bounds. Take the one at home now. People aren't allowed to go and fish in it when they want to.'

'Not anybody?'

'Oh yes, the owner comes up in the spring with his friends, and people can fish if they pay enough. Most people at home couldn't afford to do that, though.'

'So they never fish their own river?' Stretton sounded incredulous.

'Well, as a matter of fact,' Donald conceded, 'some of them

do. Like some of us come to this river although it's out of bounds. And it's all the more exciting because it's forbidden. Half the fun is not to get caught.'

Even sitting quite still, it was oppressively hot in their black clothes under the streaming sun. There was not a breath of wind.

'Look here,' said Stretton, 'can you swim? I vote we bathe.'

'Do you think we'll get caught?' Donald's thoughts had taken wing to one of Neil's poaching expeditions.

'You'll be in the soup anyway if you're caught here, so you may just as well enjoy yourself while you're about it. I've never seen any of the prefects in these parts myself.' And without further ado Stretton began to take off his clothes.

Donald followed his example, but slowly, hesitantly. He was waiting to see whether Stretton would undress completely, and he was not long in finding out.

When he and Angus had played together as children, the two boys had always turned their backs to each other secretively when they wanted to relieve themselves, and Donald had never seen the private parts of another person until he went to his prep school. And although he had reached the age of puberty before he left there, he still saw only the spectacle of naked children, to which he had grown accustomed. So it came as a shock to him when he first entered the shower rooms at his House at Stellmore, and found himself in close proximity to men stark naked, for so the older boys appeared to him. A few of them had hair on their chests. He was horribly embarrassed, but with such a crowd of boys around it was not so difficult to hide his feelings.

He had never been alone with anyone naked until Stretton removed every shred of his clothing, folded it neatly on the bank, slipped down the roots in the river, and swam across it. On the opposite side there was a small beach of gravel and rich soil formed by the bend in the river. Stretton waded up to it, and stood facing Donald. He formed the centre-piece of an enchanting picture, dappled by the shadows of a single tree on the bank, cows cropping on the green slope behind.

'Why are you taking so long?' he called. 'It's not cold.'

Donald flung off his remaining garments and followed. When he walked up the beach to his companion, he found himself staring at Stretton from head to foot. Then the laughter burst out of him as though it had been bottled up all his life. This was how all the animals saw one another, birds and fish and cattle. He was one with the whole living creation.

His laughter continued until he saw Stretton look down, and he did the same. They both had erections. Now it was Stretton's turn to laugh, while Donald felt as though an ice-cube had run down his spine. He glanced back at the wooded bank behind him and imagined it filled with prefects. Suppose anyone could see them now.

'Don't worry,' Stretton tried to reassure him. 'It's perfectly natural. All the other animals are the same. Haven't you seen them?' He trotted back through the shallow water, kicking up drops of it that turned to diamonds behind him in the air, still erect. Not so Donald as he followed. He thought of Sodom and Gomorrah and wondered whether he would be turned into a pillar of salt.

Where the water grew deeper and the current more sluggish they swam and splashed and floundered until Donald's inhibitions had been laid to rest. But there were elements in this adventure that brought back memories of that day with Angus at the point once more, and with them the sense of foreboding that they never failed to engender.

'Shouldn't we be getting back?' he asked. 'How long have we been here?'

'I'll look at my watch,' said Stretton, and he swam to where the roots fell into deep water, hauled himself out, and fumbled with his clothing.

'Good heavens, it's five o'clock,' he called. Only an hour to get back for chapel. But surely it wouldn't take as long as that.

'Do you think we can make it?' Donald asked. Stretton looked thoughtful as he pulled on his shirt over his wet skin.

'We can easily get there in time. It won't take much more than three quarters of an hour if we walk fast. The trouble is, I can't remember whether day-boys have to attend evening service this Sunday or not.' He paused to reflect as he adjusted his tie. 'Of course I could go home and find out, but then I might not make it in time.' He wriggled into his trousers, thinking the matter over in silence.

'I know,' he decided. 'I'll come along anyway just to make sure. You mightn't find the quickest way by yourself.' As soon as they were fully dressed once more in top hat and tails, they made off with long strides.

As they came through the gate at the far corner of the College site, the chapel bell began to toll. They had timed it perfectly. The bell rang for five minutes before services, and already a procession of boys was beginning to move in from the Houses on the fringe of the school grounds that were more than five minutes' walk from the chapel. The stream of little black figures presented a mournful sight, gathering for the orisons of another weekend. But Donald had survived too great a variety of hazards on this delicious day to feel mournful. On the contrary, he asked himself whether this was not the way Neil felt, returning from a successful foray to the broch pool.

They left their top hats outside on the grass and passed under the arch of the Victorian gothic porch. The chapel's faint aroma of wood varnish and the throbbing notes of the organ caught Donald's senses in the sanctity of an approach to God that was foreign to him. His mother was Episcopalian, and had given him godparents, but he had always attended the Presbyterian church in his village before he went away to prep school. And the little chapel there had been far more like the church at home than this sombre gothic building.

Stretton strode ahead up the aisle without another word to his pew further ahead. The boys did not face God in order of age, character or cricketing ability, but in form order. Before God alone intelligence was given this recognition, as though the authorities could not be sure whether the Almighty agreed with the other values which the mid-Victorians had imposed on the ancient grammar schools of England. The sixth form sat right in front, below the great altar, and Stretton sat two pews ahead of Donald, near the back. The consequence of this arrangement was that the boys of all the different Houses were intermingled like cards in a pack, rather than in their different suits.

Donald tried to compose his mind, but behind the organ notes it slipped away to river banks that were partly those at home and partly those he had just left. And his companion was Angus until suddenly he flung off his clothes, and then it was Stretton. Had he been wicked? At the morning service the singing was loud and cheerful, but there was something mysterious about the evening one. It was more hushed and sad, coloured by slow, imploring hymns like *Abide with Me* and with thoughts of the first bell on Monday morning.

From the back, the choir shuffled up the aisle in white surplices. How thankful Donald had been when he failed in his voice test because his voice was breaking. It would have been terrifying to take part in this weekly ritual in surplice and cassock, and to sit there under the great cross on the altar. Each chorister bowed to it before he took his seat, some casually with a nod, others rather self-consciously, a few with a low, fearful sweep. It was as though they feared that God himself might be hiding behind the altar, cane in hand, waiting to punish the sins of Sodom and Gomorrah.

The padre began to intone the words of the liturgy and the long cadences filled Donald's mind with a sense of magic. Who would give the sermon tonight? Often the Headmaster did, although he was not in holy orders. He had a little military moustache and still used his army rank, and his sermons were dictatorial and often made Donald feel uncomfortable. He was in the chapel but not in the seat he would have been occupying if he intended to give the sermon. There Donald saw another member of the staff who was a parson, an earnest man called Egerton who taught modern languages as well as divinity. He was considered a wet by the boys, and you could often hear the uproar in his classroom from two rooms away.

The time came for Egerton to mount the pulpit. One by one, fatefully, he climbed its steps, notes in hand. What advice would they contain, what words of comfort, what reflections on Holy Writ? Donald watched the sheets as they were spread out under the little shaded lamp. Then the earnest voice, in the name of the Father and of the Son and of the Holy Ghost, delivered its message.

'Tonight I wish to take advantage of the absence of certain boys among you to make a plea on their behalf. Try not to despise the day-boys.' The preacher paused. 'The world, you will find, is full of day-boys.'

Amid the general stir Donald drew in his feet as though they had touched something hot. He looked round furtively. There were empty places in the pews where the day-boys sat. This was not one of the Sundays on which they were obliged to attend evening chapel. But Stretton sat two pews in front of him, motionless. Were his ears sunburnt like that, or had they gone pink? Donald tried to attend as Egerton enlarged on the

55

text that we should all love one another, especially those less privileged than ourselves.

At last the sermon was over, and the last hymn, and the Blessing. The choir glided out, then all the other boys, in pairs from the pews either side of the aisle. Donald had reached a self-conscious age, and he sometimes felt embarrassed as he walked out under the eyes of the row of masters at the back of the chapel in their raised pew. But tonight he had no thought for himself, only for Stretton. He looked around for him as he picked up his top hat from the grass, and noticed him setting off across the cricket fields, all by himself. Donald was relieved that he did not need to confront him.

'Hunter!' It was Hobson, the head fag in his study, coming up behind him.

'Were you walking across the site with a day-boy before chapel?'

'Yes.' Perhaps Hobson was going to say something apologetic. You could easily misjudge people for stupid reasons.

'You don't mean to tell me you'd been for a walk with a day-boy.'

'Yes, well, I met him while I was out.'

'Can't you see you're letting the House down, Hunter?' He spoke more in sorrow than in anger. 'You want to brace yourself up.'

4

The Speech Day weekend arrived. Every available room in every hotel in the town and the surrounding countryside was booked, well in advance, by the parents of the boys. Quite early on Saturday the first cars swept into the school grounds through the gates opposite Donald's House, for this great social event of the year. On the steps of the House casual groups stood watching, moved off and reformed, with an air of unconcern. Excitement showed only in the fitfulness of the talk and the feet that kicked restlessly at the steps.

A car would draw up at the curb, and a boy would detach himself in a leisurely way from his companions to greet his parents. His manner impressed the need for formality on his parents before he reached them, in front of the eyes that watched from the House entrance and the windows. One or two of the parents leapt from their cars with a most unseemly display of affection. Bad show. Perhaps the father had not been to a public school himself.

Donald had just come out to the porch when one of these incidents occurred, and he realized how important it would be to meet his father and mother somewhere else if ever they came to a Speech Day. He walked back inside, up the dark passage to his study, and sat down at his desk. Only Hobson was still in there, tinkering with his white cricket boot.

By now Donald wished very much that his parents were coming after all, whether they brought the car or not. He would just go with them wherever they suggested, and talk about everyone at home.

'Your people coming for Speech Day?' Hobson was looking up from his cricket boot. He had treated Donald with aloof kindness ever since evening chapel on the previous Sunday, and had gone to the trouble of telling him one or two things that he ought to know.

'They live too far away,' Donald replied, then added quickly, 'but I expect they'll come next time.'

'Where do you live?'

'The north of Scotland.' Once he'd said Sutherland, but found they thought he meant Sunderland.

'Rotten luck,' sympathized Hobson. 'My people are in India, but I've an uncle coming to see me instead. Haven't you any relatives who live nearer?'

'Not near enough,' said Donald, though the question made him think speculatively about Godfather Jones, who was often in the south.

'Rotten luck,' said Hobson again, returning to explore the inner sole of his cricket boot for the nail that had been bothering him.

Did Hobson mean that it was rotten luck to live in the north of Scotland? Or living there, to be at school here? He longed to ask Hobson whether he had ever been to India, where his parents lived. But that would have been cheeky. 'Lift' they called it at Stellmore. He hadn't understood what was meant the first time he was warned not to be 'lifty', especially as he had only asked a question that he would have thought to be ordinary good manners until then. What a lot there was to learn. Restlessly Donald left his desk and went back to watch the parents arriving, standing a little apart from the groups on the House steps.

Some of the parents arrived on foot, walking from the station to the bridge that spanned the river, and up the slope beyond. Donald noticed one of them, a wispy figure in black, looking weary from her climb. Her son ran down the House steps to greet her, and he was a prefect. He put his arm round her waist and they sauntered through the school gates, laughing to one another. It must be all right if you were a prefect. Donald watched the prefect and his mother in black until they were lost in the gathering crowd of bright moving figures. Then he followed.

It was convenient to belong to a House so near the school gates if you were in a hurry for games or chapel or work. Walking between their red brick pillars you soon reached the College centre, the great field now used for cricket round which the hall, the chapel, the library and all the other buildings had been planted at different times during the last century and a half. Much larger than the rest and at some distance from them stood the long, tall block of classrooms, the origin and symbol of the public school that had grown up here when the original grammar school vanished from the town. Between each of these buildings were lawns, occasional trees and gravel paths, and converging upon them from all the Houses on the fringe of the College site were parents with their children, moving slowly in the heat.

They had come to attend chapel, to listen to speeches in the great hall, and to watch the cricket match. They had also come to be seen, and to consort with the other parents who were likewise paying for their boys to be educated at this exclusive school. The benefits in which they were investing would accrue to their offspring throughout their lives, and it was natural that they should wish to pay this visit of inspection at intervals.

Donald wandered across the road, through the school gates, and in the direction of the hall. He had never in his life seen such a multitude, such a galaxy of dresses and hats. His prep school had sometimes mustered most of the parents of its fifty boys. Here were the back-up forces of an army of over five hundred. Spell-bound by the colour, the magnificence, the graceful movement, he suddenly found himself gazing full into the eyes of a tall woman in a long blue dress. She was all on her own, looking around for someone, when her eyes met those of Donald. They were blue like her dress and so was the sapphire on her finger, as she held the wide brim of her hat in the breeze. She was beautiful, and her smile was beautiful as she opened her mouth to speak to him.

'Are you looking for someone too?' Donald longed to stay with her, but suppose she were the mother of a prefect, or a day-boy? He looked round in a panic.

'No, it's all right,' he mumbled, and with a last reluctant glance at that merry face he dived away through the crowd.

It was a hot afternoon to spend listening to the speeches in such a crowded hall. Over a thousand were accommodated in it, the boys wedged up in the gallery at the back, their parents on hard little wooden chairs below them. Squeezed into his corner at the rear of the gallery, Donald could see the Headmaster on the distant platform, swinging his pince-nez on its chain between thumb and forefinger as he had a habit of doing in the chapel pulpit during his sermons, except when he adjusted it to his nose with a flourish to read something. Donald could not have known that the man sitting two places away from him was the one peer on the school's governing body, and he did not recognize the personage who sat between them as Stanley Baldwin, the Prime Minister.

The speeches began. The acoustics of the hall were extremely poor and, cramped in his corner, Donald felt too hot and bored to attend closely to what was said from the distant platform. Instead, he began to work out a plan of escape. As soon as the speeches were over, and while everyone was watching the cricket match, he would return to the river where he had looked for Glendower's oak. He might even make a detour by way of Stretton's farm, in case he was about. He felt that he owed him an apology, though he didn't know how to express it.

This was the problem that absorbed him while the Headmaster outlined the school's problems to parents and boys, and described its purposes, and the way in which they were being fulfilled. The Headmaster's voice made only a distant hum, interrupted occasionally by a distant 'pock' sound from the batsman in the field outside. Every time the sound 'pock' disturbed the drone from the platform, Donald's plan advanced a step further, because it interrupted his day-dreams. He would call at the Stretton home and say hullo in passing. Why shouldn't he do that? Anyone could do it at home.

The Prime Minister rose. He lent on a stick and turned on his audience a look of candid good-nature. It was an expression that had helped him to earn a reputation of immense trustworthiness, and had won him an untold number of votes. Mr Baldwin began to speak. He spoke of England, what a great country this was, and of the youth of England in whose keeping the heritage of England would rest one day. Donald, who was not accustomed to hearing his country spoken of as England, began to count the number of times he heard the word spoken. Was he now an English youth? Pock. He remembered his first term at his (six) prep school, his huge popularity from the first moment the other boys heard his Highland speech. They were always asking him (seven) for stories about funny incidents at home. Pock.

'Come along, tell us another.' And they would roar with

60

laughter when he finished. But after a few terms he could speak like all the other boys. They never made such a fuss (eight) of him after that, and they didn't ask him for any more stories. Pock: followed by a cheer that nearly drowned the Prime Minister's words. Once Donald tried to tell another story without being asked, but he got muddled over the details and somebody told him to shut up. And Stretton said he didn't sound as though he came from the far north. Could he call himself English yet?

'. . . and so let us pray that the youth of England will always keep the torch of freedom shining brightly as an example to the world, and that your sons will continue to learn the great English qualities of decency and leadership in this ancient school.'

Handkerchiefs were raised surreptitiously to moist eyes as the Prime Minister brought his catalogue of simple yet profound truths to its conclusion. Or perhaps it would be more true to say that he cut it short, after observing out of the corner of his eye that the Headmaster had ceased to swing his pince-nez in time with its cadences, and was consulting his watch. The expression of beneficence was turned once more upon the sea of grateful faces. There was a stir. The Prime Minister had finished and was sitting down. A great sound of applause filled the hall. Then the headmaster, swinging his pince-nez once more, rose to his feet, collected together a little nosegay of the statesman's choicest aphorisms, and handed them back to him.

'Loyalty to King and Empire . . . Pock . . . Leading in the march of progress . . . preserving all that is best in the English (twelve) way of life.' The little military moustache on the Headmaster's rather short upper lip quivered over the unerring selection.

Now everyone seemed to have reached the end of their patience at the same moment, packed together on such hard little seats in such a temperature. They moved to ease their limbs, and many of them fanned themselves with hats and hands, and there was the politest of stampedes to the exits. By the time Donald's turn came to file out of the gallery most of the parents were already on the lawn beside the cricket pitch, and while some turned to watch the game, others hovered as near as they could to the person of the Prime Minister. Leaning on his stick, he continued the stream of portentous remarks that he had discontinued in the hall, smiling benignly.

'. . . where the English character is formed . . .' Donald heard as he passed the outer rim of the silent hoverers. He saw the mother in black striding away with her prefect son. She was talking with great animation while he smiled, and Donald was soothed by the assurance with which they ignored both the cricket match and the Prime Minister as they walked right between these competing distractions. Then he noticed the lady in blue again and was thankful that he had not been caught talking to her, because her son was nothing less than the head boy of the College himself. Donald would never have lived it down, being as 'lifty' as that.

Now for the plan. But he wasn't sure how to slip away from a school match, on Speech Day of all occasions, with so many eyes on the lookout. The prefect with his mother had done it certainly, and Donald supposed that anyone might leave the College grounds with his parents. He gazed around wondering which might be the safest escape route, and saw Hobson with his uncle not twenty yards away. They were not speaking to one another and did not look as though they had much to talk about. As each stared about him, Hobson noticed Donald and gave a cheerful smile and a wave. He felt immensely grateful, but turned in the opposite direction lest Hobson should witness his escape. In doing so he came face to face with Stretton, who was standing just behind his parents. His father was large and freckled, and his mother was surveying the crowd tolerantly but distantly. They might have been residents of some seaside resort, facing a bank holiday crowd.

'Hullo, Hunter, on your own again?'

'Yes.' The memory of the chapel sermon sent the blood to his head.

'Then why not come home with us? We're just leaving, and the car's parked just up the road from your House.' Stretton turned to his parents.

'This is Hunter,' he said. 'It's his first term.' Donald shook hands with both of them.

'Yes, do come along,' said Stretton's father heartily, and his mother gave him an encouraging smile.

Donald glanced quickly over his shoulder. Hobson was still staring at him but he wasn't smiling any more. His expression was stony. Donald panicked.

'Thanks very much but my people are arriving soon,' he brought out in a rush.

'Oh that's fine. Well, I think we'll leave now. Too many people.'

Donald stood quite still until they were out of sight. Pock. Then the batsman was caught. But Donald did not turn to see why everyone cheered. He walked straight back to his House, no longer caring whether he was observed. His study was empty, the sun shining harshly on a railway poster above his desk, the green cotton curtains and the leaves outside the window swishing like the blue skirt of the beautiful lady holding the brim of her hat as she searched for her son. The distant sounds of the match could be heard here, as bat hit ball and an occasional cheer rang out. Donald slumped down in his seat and remained there, his head between his arms on the desk. Pock. The system was achieving results almost as fast as the Prime Minister prophesied them. Donald was learning to play the game.

Angus heard of his return almost as soon as he reached home for his summer holidays at the beginning of August. But he had not seen him yet by the time he arranged to sail with his brothers Neil and Jack to the island. Neil had returned from the fishing since his father's death, and while Jack continued to work on the roads, he and Angus combined fishing for lobsters with work on the family croft. Neil also did some gillying with the folk who came up to fish the river and the lochs.

They had bought an old engine for their boat, which they kept by the little jetty at the river mouth. But on this day Neil had sailed it round to the Port to put the lobster creels aboard before taking these to drop around the island. As he was shifting them from beside the upturned hulk, Angus suddenly remembered Donald.

'I never asked Donnie would he like to come to the island,' he told his brother. 'I promised him the first time we went to the island we would take him, and now he's back.'

'Jack will be waiting for us at the jetty,' Neil objected.

'I'll take the bike. Then I'll be back with Donnie in no time at all. Or he could join Jack at the jetty.' Neil was over ten years his senior, but since Angus left school Neil had taken the trouble to defer to him as an adult whenever possible. With only the slightest trace of annoyance, Neil said, 'Hurry then.' The weather had been stormy of late, but now the wind had subsided and there was a dead calm. Neil was impatient to drop his creels. Also, he planned to bring back some sheep from the island, which would make the boat rather crowded with Donald in it as well.

Angus rode as fast as he dared among the deepening pot-holes of the side road, and let rip with a roar when he reached the main one so that the sound echoed from the rocks beside the glebe fields. He drove more sedately as he approached Donald's gate, where he saw him standing on the lawn.

'Hullo, Donnie,' he called. 'So you got back.'

'Hullo, Angie.' Donald ran forward to shake his hand. 'I'm sorry I haven't been over to see you yet but I was meaning to.'

'I'm sorry to be in such a hurry, but we're just off to the island in Neil's boat. Will you come?'

Donald turned to look at the island lying out beyond the river mouth, green in the sunshine. Then he inspected the gravel path, kicking at it with a toe. It would have been simple to explain that the Joneses were coming to lunch, whom he had not seen for a year, or to ask his parents if they thought it would be all right for him to go to the island and see them another time. But a confused sequence of images was passing through his mind, Angus standing naked on the gravel beach the other side of the river, calling, 'Hurry up and come over': Angus standing with Stretton's parents in the Speech Day crowds, saying, 'Why don't you come back with us?': Hobson in the background with his uncle, shouting so that everyone could hear, 'Can't you see you're letting the House down, Hunter?' Donald looked up.

'I don't think I'll come this time,' he said. 'Thanks awfully for asking me all the same.'

The boys exchanged looks as strangers do when they suspect they have met before. Then Angus gave a kick to start the engine of his bike.

'Well, I'll have to be off,' he said. 'I mustn't keep Jackie and Neil waiting. Cheerio.'

By the time he reached the cliff above the port, there was Neil's boat filled with lobster creels and lines and dark glass floats all in a tangle. Round about it in the sheltered water square boxes floated, for keeping the lobsters fresh until they could be despatched to the south. Neil was bent over the stern, tinkering with the engine with greasy experimental fingers. He looked up when Angus shouted to him.

'The divil,' he called. 'But she'll go now.' Angus started down the ruinous path, sending loose stones clattering on to the old sea wall at the bottom.

The muddle in the boat was a projection of Neil's character, an assertion that order and method are inessentials. His engine, once it was started, never broke down, and it would not have occurred to Neil that he might catch more lobsters if he stowed his gear neatly. The moods of the weather were the essential things to understand, and these Neil could anticipate with uncanny foresight.

'Donnie couldn't come?' he called over his shoulder as Angus trotted down the shingle. Neil was among the few of his age who preferred to speak in Gaelic, in which he was most loquacious. But his younger brothers had crossed the language frontier, so although they could understand his Gaelic, he spoke to them in the tongue they used. This he did tersely and without ornament.

He gave a tug at the cord that started the motor just as Angus slid, groping, amongst the disorderly tackle. He stooped to tidy it, one hand on the gunwhale, while the little craft rolled and tonked out into the bay. Beyond the jetty the sea sucked and gushed at the rocks, dazzling white and very clear green. Even in such clam weather it heaved with the pulse of the north Atlantic. Beyond the point the sea turned blue and although it remained just as smooth, its undulations gave warning of the frightening strength slumbering in the depths of that mighty ocean.

As they rounded the headland that separated them from the river mouth, they saw the figure of Jack, waiting on its jetty.

'You managed,' called Neil.

'No bother,' Jack shouted back. In the distance behind Jack, Angus saw Donald standing on the slope above his home, watching them. He waved and Donald returned his greeting.

'I could have persuaded Donnie to come,' Angus said to Neil. 'I'm sure he wanted to. I didn't give him time to think.'

'There was hardly room for him,' Neil replied. 'Especially

when we have the sheep.' Jack leapt aboard, Neil turned the boat about, and they were on their way to the island.

A dead sheep floated by in the water: it must have fallen off one of the cliffs. A seal's head appeared, dark and shiny as one of the glass floats, then it disappeared and a tail-fin flicked the surface in its place. A skein of geese flew overhead and alighted on the island, close to the deserted croft houses. They fed themselves in one of the parks, which looked as square and green as if the land there were still tended. Angus stood with the first lobster creel ready to throw overboard, gazing at the solid stone empty buildings. How could people have lived on that patch of pasture and bare rock, with two miles of sea to cross in little open boats by oar and sail?

'Mam was saying some of the islanders never dared to make the journey at all,' he remarked, 'and only came to the mainland to be buried.' Angus looked back at the scattered townships along the coast, the headlands jutting out to sea between them, the little white houses, the great mountains behind. This was his world as the islanders had seen it and a wonderful sight it was. Gazing at it from such an unfamiliar perspective, he experienced an emotion he had never known before. He felt a longing to return. He wouldn't have minded if Neil had turned the boat round before he had so much as set foot on the island.

But it continued to tonk its way forward until it was close to steep basalt cliffs, quite unlike those of his home surroundings, to where the blue sea became flecked with white again as it gnawed at the rocks. Neil slowed the engine and they began to toss the creels overboard, one after another.

'See if we don't haul her in empty,' Neil prophesied gloomily as Jack paid out a line. 'Wicked creatures, that lobsters.' He stared incredulously into the deep clear water, as though unable to comprehend the obstinacy of lobsters.

The island was about a mile long and less in breadth, and almost its entire circumference was girt with towering cliffs. The boat rocked slowly past *Uamh an Latha* and *Uamh na h-Oidhche*, the Caves of Day and Night, from which on this still day they could hear a deep-throated boom. Neil turned his boat at the chasm in which the fish had been hung to dry in former times. It was a narrow chimney in the rock up which wind and spume rushed with a whistling sound, and beside it a smooth ledge ran into the sea, a favourite haunt of the grey seal after which the island was named, *Eilean nan Ròn*. Several of them flopped into the water as though resenting the invasion of their privacy. But one sat on, staring the intruders out of countenance.

Passing a more serrated ledge from which dozens of sandpipers fluttered in alarm, they came to the landing-place. It consisted merely of some concrete steps on a narrow protrusion of rock, altogether unprotected from rough seas. Jack crouched in the bows to fasten the boat to one of the worn and rusted rings. The engine spluttered to a stop, and the three brothers were left suddenly in the utter silence of the deserted island.

'She's fast now,' called Jack, but apart from that none of them seemed inclined to break the stillness that surrounded them.

They climbed the steep steps and threaded their way along the path to the top, a narrow defile below which the sea heaved on either hand, until they reached the central basin of grass. The geese were gone. The lines of division between the crofts showed more faintly on the ground than they had done in the distance. Neil and Jack made off to the higher ground to the right in search of their sheep, towards the dangerous cliffs from which they fell from time to time, tempted by the succulent tufts on their ledges. Angus sauntered in the other direction, exploring this abandoned world for the first time.

He stopped at the first house he came to. It was built of stone and slates, larger than his own home, with V-shaped storm windows upstairs instead of sky-lights in the roof like the one in his bedroom. The stone must all have come from the mainland by boat with the slates, since the island rock was volcanic. Angus turned the knob of the door and walked in. The flag-stoned kitchen had a musty smell and it felt chilly in there out of the sun, but quite dry. There was no furniture, only a discoloured Gaelic Bible that still lay on the window ledge. And by the fireplace a calendar still hung, its pages torn off up to September. That was the month of the year in which the last old people had been taken off the island.

Angus surveyed the kitchen, so like others on the mainland, the calendar and the Bible, its only ornaments, such scanty and impersonal memorials to the people who had once lived here. Yet the lettering on the old grave-stones in the cemetery behind the bay became illegible in a comparable way until little or nothing could be read of it any more. Even the writing on his father's stone would become faint with time, although now it appeared so sharp and enduring.

The sense of isolation in that empty kitchen brought to mind the words of the Minister when he said it was better to live safe from all the snares and temptations of this wicked world. Angus was becoming acutely aware how compulsive these snares and temptations could be, though he had as yet scant idea of their range. He thought of the people here who had been able to count their days in this vale of woe, immune from the wiles of the Devil, as they tore the pages from their calendar, quietly reading about the Elect in the Word of God as it was written in the Bible on the window ledge. Through the window they could see heaven as a great land of mountains with the sun circling behind them, across the water.

He tiptoed out of the house as though afraid to disturb the silence, and shut the door carefully behind him. There was no church on the island, but across the fields stood the school, a single room built on to the end of the teacher's house. The people had met there to worship when a Minister visited the island. Perhaps they held dances there too. But no, they had all been members of the Free Church and would not have danced. No snares, no temptations, just church meetings in the schoolhouse, and prayer meetings at home. Long slow psalms and solemn prayers, all in Gaelic, as they had at his father's funeral. Angus thought of Christine, whose parents were such narrow Free Church members. If his mind could switch from his dead father to her so quickly, the Devil was never far away.

Angus reached the schoolroom. Its door had been left open so that the sheep could enter, and now their droppings lay so thick among the upturned desks that the door would no longer shut. He found the hole he had been told about where the children used to hide the cane. It was burnt into the wooden panelling beside the window. There was a sum on the blackboard, but its answers were concealed among the sheep droppings. What did it matter any more?

He wandered out into the sunlight again, away from the houses, down to the spring from where they had drawn their water. The track was still well-defined. He knelt down beside it and took a deep cool draught from between his cupped hands, and then sat down beside it to wait for the others. The spring alone still poured out its clear stream with undiminished vitality. It came out of the ground a little to the right of the landing-place, and poured down a steep gully to the island's one little sandy cove. This was the only place where a boat could be beached, though even when it was upturned at the very highest point beneath the cliffs it was not altogether safe from a storm.

Once the islanders had gone out to retrieve the bodies from a sailing ship wrecked in a gale on the rocks. They had left them in this cove overnight, covered by sails. Looking down from where Angus sat, they had seen the corpses of the drowned sailors lit by phosphorescent foam as though candles were lit at their heads and feet. So the place was called the Bay of the Candles in Gaelic. Neil had told Angus the story as though he really believed that supernatural lights had burned for the dead men.

'Come along, Angie, we're ready to go back with the sheep.'

Neil and Jack had only three with them, bleating and trying to make off in all directions, hard to manage without a dog. Angus helped to run them down to the cove, where they tied their legs. As soon as this had been done the sheep became perfectly passive, and lay there as though they had come to relax on the beach of their own volition. They gave a few convulsive wriggles as they were put aboard the boat, and then their patient and adaptable natures reasserted themselves.

So early in the afternoon the three brothers sailed home to their dinners. At the port beside the bay they untied the sheep and shooed them up its steep path. But they had no sooner topped the summit of the headland when Neil signalled to his brothers to stop, without saying a word. He was staring at a green patch of the inlet beyond, a rocky indentation of the kind that people called a *geò*. On the flat field behind, the geese from the island were feeding while one of them kept watch.

'You just wait here,' whispered Neil when his brothers had edged up to him. 'I'll get the gun, and then we'll have one of yon. Just you keep standing there where they can see you and don't move at all.' With that he slunk back below the summit of the headland and round to his house by a route that kept him always out of sight of the geese. Jack and Angus remained motionless.

The geese looked up now and again, and a few would show occasional signs of restlessness before returning to their meal. But while the brothers almost held their breath, no general panic infected the flock to send them wheeling off in search of a safer pasture.

Then Jack and Angus saw a sight that made them heave with suppressed laughter. Neil was returning with his gun, making his way down the far side of the marshy ground beyond the football field. First he took advantage of the broken terrain but next he was on his hands and knees, and finally he was slithering on his stomach. He looked up at his brothers with a comic expression of enquiry, as though it was past belief that the birds could still be there. Meanwhile the geese still gave them an occasional indifferent glance.

A shot rang out. Neil had raised himself on his elbows, bringing himself within sight of the birds for just long enough to take aim. They flew off urgently, except for two of them which lay where they had been standing before.

'By Jove,' exclaimed Bill Jones, 'I wonder who that was.' They were relaxing after luncheon in Donald's home, discussing preparations for the grouse shooting that was to commence on the twelfth August, in a week's time. The Joneses had kept less frequent residence in the north since his election to Parliament at the last general election. He had been chosen to stand for a safe seat in one of the residential areas outside London whose inhabitants lived in rows of variegated houses with small, well-kept gardens and names that commemorated, in many cases, their owners' distant places of origin. Jones was conscientious in the discharge of his duties, for which he had been rewarded already with a knighthood.

He looked out of the window of the Hunters' drawing-room, the concern he felt for the safety of his salmon now transferred to his grouse.

'The shot came from the far side of the bay, I would say,' said Captain Hunter without moving from his chair.

'What the devil do they think they're up to?' boomed Sir William. 'Do you mind if I borrow your binoculars? I'm going out to take a look.' He hurried from the room, took the binoculars from their peg in the hall, leapt into his car and sped to the high point of the road above the village.

'As I was saying,' Lady Jones hastened to pour into the

opportune silence left by her husband's departure, 'all this living in three places at once is a perfect martyrdom. Just before we came up, I lost the chance of a first night at Covent Garden.'

'Was it something you particularly wanted to hear?' asked Mrs Hunter.

'Oh I've no idea. But Lady Surbiton invited me and the only thing I could possibly have worn was down in the country.'

'How disappointing,' murmured Mrs Hunter. 'You're so fond of opera, too.'

'I simply love all music,' Lady Jones confirmed, 'though of course nothing more than the sound of the bagpipes. Not indoors, I mean. Lord Charterford had someone playing at a dinner last year and it was a horrid noise. Down there they just don't understand.' A fey note entered her voice, the kind described in novels she read about happenings in mountain mists.

Donald had been sitting quietly all this time, listening abstractedly to the talk about the great world of the south. It was only when Sir William Jones burst in again that he focused clearly on what was being said in the room.

'It was Magnus's three sons,' he announced triumphantly. 'I saw them through the glasses walking up to their house. They were carrying two large birds and a gun.'

'They must have killed two with one shot,' observed Captain Hunter. 'Good firing. What sort of birds? Any grouse down there?'

'Much larger than grouse. Sort of light brown colour.'

'Geese,' said Captain Hunter.

'How dreadful,' exclaimed Lady Jones. 'Fancy killing those beautiful creatures. Can't you stop them, Bill? They might become extinct.' The prospect brought a lump to her throat.

'Angus and the others were over on the island,' Donald remarked inconsequentially.

'I wonder whether I ought to stop them from going there,' said Sir William. 'They've no right to. I paid compensation for the crofts when the people left. Anyway I must find out whether they have a licence for that gun. There are too many people around here with not enough to do. They ought to go south and look for work.'

'With three million unemployed there already?' asked Mrs

Hunter.

'You've got a point there, Katrine,' Sir William conceded with the ready sympathy that was never far below the surface of his nature. On the other hand, his sympathy for Mrs Hunter's opinions was by now warmer than his enthusiasm for the Highlands, which had lasted about as long as is customary in such cases, and had been eroded further by his parliamentary commitments. Indeed, he would probably have sold his Highland estate by now but for his wife's romantic attachment. As often as he heard her expressing her love for the bens and glens in London society, and she grew ever more eloquent on the subject, he postponed his intention to rid himself of what had become an encumbrance. Lady Jones was perhaps aware of the threat to her dream world, for she responded quickly to criticism of its inhabitants from her husband, even when she had just uttered them herself.

'Come along,' she said to him, rising. 'It's time to go.'

'Quite right, my dear,' Sir William replied energetically. 'Some of us lead busy lives, and I hope useful ones.' So they said goodbye and drove off down the strath.

'Nice lad Donald's turning out,' Sir William reflected over the steering wheel. 'That was interesting, what he told us about the Prime Minister's visit to Stellmore. We must go and see Donald next speech day. Mustn't forget he's my godson.'

After waving goodbye to her guests, Mrs Hunter went back into the drawing-room, where she found Donald sitting alone. Captain Hunter had retired to his favourite chair in the study.

'Why didn't you say they were going to the island after Angus called this morning?' she asked him gently. 'You didn't need to stay here. You could easily have gone and seen the Joneses another time.'

'Angie did ask me to go, but I said I didn't want to,' Donald replied reflectively. The spectre of Hobson appeared in his mind's eye again, this time fiddling with his cricket boot and saying, 'You live in the north of Scotland? Rotten luck.' Donald sat securely shut in his chair and eyed his mother defensively. And seeing him there, not exactly unhappy, but locked away from her, she came and sat on the arm of his chair, as though in a desperate effort to make contact with him again.

'But Donnie,' she said, 'you always wanted to visit the island.' When he made no response she went on, 'Tell me what you would really like to do most.'

As though cornered, Donald rose and stood at bay with his back to the mantelpiece.

'I would like to go somewhere else for my holidays,' he replied. He had taken to his heels, and was now running away from the refuges once so familiar and secure. His mother caught her breath and said nothing.

'Couldn't I go to some of the other places the boys at Stellmore talk about? You've never taken me to London.' It was like an accusation.

'I'll talk to Daddy about it,' Mrs Hunter said in a level voice.

5

Captain Hunter greeted the proposal with extreme displeasure.

'What nonsense,' he wheezed from the depths of his chair. He was becoming more inactive as his breathing difficulty increased. 'Why should Donald want to visit London?' Mrs Hunter gave Donald a modified version of her husband's words, as she so often did, and the subject was not mentioned again.

But soon afterwards Captain Hunter was compelled to spend some weeks under observation in an Edinburgh hospital, and within the year it had been decided that they must abandon their home on the north coast because it was too far from medical facilities. They moved to a house near the coast east of Inverness, where the climate is so mild and sunny for that latitude, and where the northern hills can still be seen beyond the Moray Firth. So Donald was already separated by this barrier from his childhood surroundings by the time he won his House colours for cricket at Stellmore, and Sir William and Lady Jones paid their long-promised visit on the following Speech Day, and invited him to stay with them in London during the summer holidays. In these circumstances Captain Hunter gave his consent.

The Houses of Parliament were not in session, but Sir William took Donald to see them, and described how he had cheered Mr Chamberlain in the chamber of the Commons when he returned from Munich, bringing peace with honour. Lady Jones gave a cocktail party at which Donald attended to her guests in a manner that filled her with approval. But it also reminded her of the other Donald whom she had known as a small boy in the romantic surroundings of the north.

'If only you could have seen him then,' she said to Lady

Charterford as Donald hovered with a tray of small confections. 'He was just like a little native in those days. Almost an aboriginal.'

She gave her brittle laugh. A cold hand clutched at Donald's heart and he almost dropped his tray.

This could still happen to him. A sight or sound would evoke a memory buried deep in his subconsciousness, filling him with a sense of loss and desolation. But it would pass, and then he would shrug off these moods of introspection. The past was past and its shadows must not be allowed to darken the present.

The present became dark enough to obscure such shadows when war broke out, a few months after Donald's eighteenth birthday. It also solved the immediate problem of his future career when he left Stellmore. He was called up into the army, so that he was already in uniform when he visited Inverness on leave in the winter of 1940. There he went to see his father in hospital and encountered Christine, also wearing a uniform. It was a strange, awkward meeting between the soldier and the nurse in the hospital corridor.

'Heavens, it's you, Donald.'

He had not even recognized her until she spoke. Although their parents had been such close neighbours at home, he had not seen her since she was a young girl. The memories flooded back, only they were not shadows this time but a light filling the shiny passage. Christine could not stay to talk.

'I'll meet you when I come off duty at six,' she said. 'At the main entrance.'

Donald walked on to his father's ward, but his thoughts were with Christine while Captain Hunter gazed proudly at Donald's uniform and asked him questions about the army. From what Donald remembered of her parents, he couldn't think how she had persuaded them to let her become a nurse. They had been so strict and censorious, so anxious to protect her from the pitfalls of this sinful world.

Donald remained with his father longer than he had intended, not because they had so much to say to one another, but because there was no point in returning home when he would be meeting Christine at six. The hospital faced the river Ness, and since the evening was dry though chilly, he strolled along its bank in his greatcoat, the darkness lit by stars above and almost as many memories, points of light, below. At last the hour arrived and Christine emerged from the hospital, almost trotting, in her cape.

'Are you hungry?' he asked her.

'I can eat here,' she replied. 'What about you?'

'There's dinner waiting for me at home. You could come too.'

Donald tried to picture his mother's reaction if he should turn up on the doorstep with Christine. Would she mind?

'Let's just go for a walk,' Christine suggested. 'There's so much to talk about and I'd like some fresh air.' Donald gazed at her searchingly before she moved into the darkness. Her hair was black, but the light behind it gave her a sort of halo and her white skin looked transparently pale. She noticed his stare and laughed.

'Yes, aren't we different?' She was not her parents' protected daughter any more but a being she had fashioned for herself. Donald became aware of her easy self-assurance and wondered how he appeared to her by contrast. He felt his uniform to be a kind of protection, though he could not have explained what it concealed or guessed whether Christine could see through it. They wandered down the river bank and over the footbridge, talking at random of earlier times until she remarked:

'I'm going home tomorrow for my holiday.'

'I would like to go back there myself,' Donald found himself saying, 'just to take a look.'

'It hasn't changed,' she replied.

They spent no more than an hour in each other's company, but before they parted Donald assured her that he would come up a couple of days after her return home.

'I expect you could stay with us,' said Christine. 'I'll tell you when you arrive off the bus.'

'It would be better maybe to stay with Angus,' Donald replied. 'If they would have me.' He was surprised to find himself slipping back into a forgotten inflection of speech. Christine paused to consider.

'That might be better,' she agreed. 'I'll tell him you're coming.' So they parted, between the river and the hospital.

A bus dropped Donald at the side-road a short walk from his home. His mother expressed surprise that he had not returned earlier but was delighted when he told her of his meeting with

76

Christine. Neither did she raise any objection when he asked if she would mind his visiting the north coast. Once upon a time, he remembered dimly, he had expected his father to understand and defend his point of view, not his mother. But he had learnt otherwise before he was introduced to *The Bacchae* of Euripides during his last year at Stellmore. He had found the play rather incomprehensible, except the ending which declared that many things in life turn out differently than we expect. This had reminded him in a flash of his earlier attitude to his parents.

On the morning of the day on which Donald was due to arrive by the afternoon bus, Christine determined to visit her aunt Betsag out on the Point. She would take the morning bus that ran along the coast road past the Point Inn, and walk out to the Point from there. She could return to the inn and catch the bus on its way back in the afternoon.

Her parents tried to veto this visit. They themselves showed little affection for Betsag, who was Christine's mother's sister and was married to a coffin-maker. A drunkard, they called him, meaning that he would not refuse a drink. They swept her through to the ben room that was never used except to receive the Minister or some equally important visitor. Here they were able to argue with Christine in the presence of a harmonium and a silver-plated tea tray that was kept in a glass cabinet. It had been left behind as a present by an eccentric lady lodger who had stayed with them for six months, writing strange poetry at night. Subsequently she had been placed in a mental hospital. But that was long ago, long enough for her tea tray to have become invested with the status of a family heirloom.

Christine too had enjoyed the occasional privilege of being invited into this room sanctified by Minister and poetess. It was here that they had seated her on the solemn occasions in the past when they had instructed her in the Rules of Life in the presence of the harmonium and the silver-plated tray. Evidently they expected the same influences to be effective once more, but they were disappointed. Christine lurched happily eastwards along the winding coast road to visit Betsag while her parents deplored that they had ever permitted her to take up nursing in Inverness.

'And she's only seventeen,' her mother reflected mournfully, pursing her lips together, 'just a child.' Her daughter meanwhile was pondering in her jolting bus on the hazards of announcing to her parents that she intended to go to the dance in the village hall that night. Then her thoughts turned to Donald, grown so large, shy and awkward, yet so genuine in his desire to return here. It was as well that she had not asked her parents whether he could stay in their home, although it contained the usual little spare bedroom off the upstairs landing. He was welcome to stay in Angie's home, and they would all meet at the dance.

The wind hit the ancient bus in great gusts. As they entered a hollow or descended the east side of a headland there would be a brief respite. But generally when the door was opened to put out a parcel or take in a passenger it would come swirling in around their ankles. On the way to the Point there were only two villages resembling Christine's, houses in some sort of a cluster on either side of the road. These lay at intervals of about eight miles. But between them at shorter intervals there were pillar boxes with gravel roads beside them that wound out of sight towards the sea. From houses they served, hidden in the ravines, shawled women had walked to the road junctions and stood waiting patiently in the wind for the bus to pass.

As soon as they had boarded it they added their quota of comment on the weather and information about people, gradually extending the links that bound all these scattered folk in a single community by the swift exchange of personal detail. But Christine's thoughts were elsewhere and anyway the people mentioned, and their affairs, were becoming increasingly strange to her by the time she stepped out into the gale at the Point Inn. Then she felt at home again as she turned towards the headland and her aunt Betsag's house.

The headland extended northwards for about three miles from the inn where Christine left the main road, and she had at least two miles to walk on a gravel path full of pot-holes. She held the knot of the scarf she wore round her head and leaned into the wind as she breasted each rise. Many of the houses on either hand were thatched, as none were in her own village. Some of the steddings were built of stone only to the height of the gable-ends, whose triangles were constructed of peats.

To the right of her were deep clefts, or geòs, in which houses sheltered among rocks and small patches of soil. The waves breaking on the cliffs beyond sent spindrift hurtling through the air and the Orkney islands in the distance were no more than a blur in the white-flecked ocean. Gradually the headland narrowed and became more barren until the sea burst over it in clouds of spray. But Christine turned aside from this sight as she took the path to her aunt's house.

Betsag came to the door looking weird with nails sticking out from between her teeth. She fumbled as she removed them, holding the door against the wind with her other hand.

'Tom is finishing a coffin,' she explained. 'Come away in. You must be starved.' Her uncle Tom had a coffin almost finished on the table in the kitchen. Sitting crouched towards the open peat fire was Tom's brother, his face turned blankly towards Christine as she entered.

'Hullo, Geordie,' she said to him with a merry smile, careful to give him priority, and his face relaxed into a faint, grateful expression of recognition. Generally Christine encountered him out of doors, recoating the house with a wash of lime, or doing something in the little garden enclosed by a dry-stone wall, or tinkering with a broken fence. If anyone came in sight he would stop the little that he was doing to stare after them until they disappeared. He never used speech, and in this weather there was nothing for him to do with his hands either. So he sat motionless by the left side of the fire and continued to stare at Christine.

'So you're finishing a coffin, Tom,' she said to her uncle as he stood, hammer in hand, the other side of the kitchen table.

'It will be another of your patients,' Tom replied with a wink. 'You keep me that busy.' He wiped the back of a hand across his brow as though to indicate the strain her nursing career was placing on the undertakers.

'Get away with you,' Christine retorted, glancing down at the deal planks. She had never set eyes on a coffin here before, though she had seen the kind they made in Inverness. She ran a finger down one of the cracks.

'Will this be all right?' she asked.

'If there is not a delay, or the weather is not too hot, my little nurse,' Tom answered. 'There have been times when it was hard for those who were carrying it. But not at this time of year.' He finished hammering in the nails that Betsag had taken out of her mouth and now handed to him. Then he lifted the coffin into a corner and they all settled down to gossip.

Tom was a large florid man with a most serious expression, and only the slightest hint of a twinkle in his eye. He was a great favourite at the dances with his fiddle, which he had learned to play from his father without ever discovering how to read a note.

'Will you be playing at our dance tonight?' Christine asked him.

'I will not,' said Tom, feigning indignation. 'They never invited me.'

'Well, play for me now. It's me that's inviting you.'

But Betsag had far too many questions to ask Christine that couldn't possibly wait while Tom played the fiddle. She must know how Christine liked the place where she stayed at the hospital, if she was happy in her work, how often she had a day off. She hung on Christine's words with a shake of her head or a sympathetic click of the tongue, and a new question whenever Christine stopped. Tom's brother looked across at her, never moving or altering his expression, and an occasional puff of wind down the chimney sent a little balloon of smoke out into the room between them.

'Put more peat on the fire,' Betsag asked him in Gaelic.

'I'm sorry you have to speak English to me,' Christine apologized quickly, though really it was not her fault. Her own parents had deliberately refrained from speaking anything but English to her at home, and she had once seen Miss Cameron the schoolteacher punish two children whom she caught speaking Gaelic in the playground. Some said she was trying to give them a better chance in life by making them speak in a language that everyone in the world understood. But others suggested that she was afraid of what they might be saying about her in a language she couldn't understand. She was extremely religious and a regular visitor to Christine's parents.

Here on the Point most people still spoke Gaelic at home, and she had heard some of them doing so on the bus and felt a wave of regret that she could not understand her own native language. It came over her again as she looked across at Geordie, carefully stacking fresh peats on the fire.

'Does he understand any English?' she asked Betsag in a low voice. She shook her head. He was even isolated from them in this way, and she was the cause of it.

Betsag noticed her embarrassment and asked another question, until in the end Christine had given wing to all the little birds caged inside her, the likes and dislikes, the pleasures and hardships of her new life, the special thoughts like white doves that she had been saving for her aunt. And when Betsag saw that they were all released, she let Christine ask about their children, the daughter in Orkney, the son on a ranch in South America, the other son in the army. She described their affairs briefly and then turned to her husband.

'It's little wonder you are not invited to the dance when you will not even take up your fiddle for a pretty girl any more.'

After the proper ritual of coaxing and protesting, Tom went to fetch his fiddle and played it, sitting on a straight chair against the wall beside his coffin, while Betsag took one large black pot from its hook above the fire, and put another in its place. Tom held the fiddle in his right hand, but it did not rest under his chin. It passed almost flat across his chest to his left shoulder-blade. And as Tom played, his brother sat quite motionless beside the fire except that one foot tapped, in perfect time, to the music.

Tom played all kinds of tunes, reels and waltzes, songs and strathspeys.

'You'll be in fine cut for the dance tonight with all these airs going round in your head,' he said to Christine as he stopped to pluck a string and tune it. The wind roared in the chimney and the little balloons of smoke from the peat fire puffed out from under the great black pot hanging above it. Betsag moved about, preparing the dinner and Geordie still kept time with his foot.

Then Christine noticed the two paper-backed volumes lying on the window ledge beside her.

'What are you reading?' she asked idly. Tom was tuning his fiddle again, balanced upright on the point of his knee.

'Betsag found them upstairs,' he answered. 'They tell how we came out to the Point.'

'But that was a long time ago, surely.'

'The same time as when your Dad's family were put off the strath and went to live on the coast.'

'They were lucky not to find themselves here,' Christine laughed. Walking out along the headland on such a stormy day, she thought it the most barren, windswept place imaginable. Tom put his fiddle against the wall and rose to pick up the two well-thumbed volumes.

'My great-grandfather was just a lad when the clearances happened in the strath, and he was an old man when all those big-shots came up to make an enquiry. And everything he told them is printed here.' He fumbled over the pages with his large clumsy fingers. 'What surprises me is how well he could express himself in English. The folk here couldn't have been using it much in them days.'

There were a few moments of silence that no one attempted to fill while the pages rustled, then Tom went back to his chair beside the fiddle.

'I will tell you what my great-grandfather said to their lordships, he said, holding a page close to his eyes rather than going to a place where he could read in a better light.

'One of the panel asked him, "Where were you brought up yourself"?' Tom tried to imitate the sonorous voice of the questioner. As Christine listened to the replies, it was as though she could hear Tom's great-grandfather himself telling the story that still dominated the folk-memory of her community.

'In the strath.'

'When did you leave the strath?'

'I left when young and came to the Point when the sheep commenced.'

'Were you old enough to remember the circumstances of the people at the time?'

'It would be a very hard heart but would mourn to see the circumstances of the people that day. He would be a very cruel man who would not mourn for the people.'

'What condition were they in before they left?'

'If you were going up the strath now you would see on both sides of it the places where the towns were. You would see a mile or half a mile between every town. There were four or five families in each of these towns, and bonny haughs between towns and hill pasture for miles, as far as they could wish to go. The people had plenty of flocks of goats, sheep, horses and cattle, and they were living happy.'

Tom's voice rose and fell like the wind singing in the chimney as he spoke with the voice of his great-grandfather. He might have been reciting poetry. Then his lordship's next question.

'Do you remember yourself quite well that these people were

comfortably off at the time?'

'Remarkably comfortable, that is what they were, with flesh and fish and butter and cheese, and fowl and potatoes and kail and milk too. There was no want of anything with them. And they had the Gospel preached to them at both ends of the strath.'

'You are quite satisfied yourself that these people were far better off than their children are now?'

'Oh yes, I am quite satisfied of that.' Then Tom's great-grandfather launched abruptly into a reminiscence in a way that startled Christine.

'The thing that frightened me when I was nearly drowned that day was this. My father and mother and my brother went away, having got notice that if anything was upon the ground at twelve o'clock they would be fined. They rose in the morning and went away with cattle, sheep, a horse, two mares, and two foals, to the place they were to live in after; and left me and my brothers who were younger sleeping in the bed. And there was a woman came in and said, "Won't you wake up? Sellar is burning at a place called Rhistog".

'We got such a fright that we started out of bed and ran down to the river, because there was a friend of ours living upon the other side, and we wished to go there for protection. I took my brother on my back and I fell, and he gripped round about my neck, and I could not rise nor move. We were both greeting, and took a fright that we would be drowned. There was a poor woman coming with her family up the strath, and she saw us and jumped into the river and swept us out of it.'

'How old were you when this happened to yourself?'

'About eleven years of age.'

'How old was your brother that you were carrying?'

'Three years of age.'

'Do you remember that a number of houses were burned at that time?'

'Oh yes, yes.'

'Many houses?'

'All from the river Owen Malloch and another river coming into the strath on the east side of the Dunvedan Burn.'

'Were the people very willing to leave the strath?'

'You would have pitied them, tumbling on the ground and greeting and tearing the ground with their hands. Any soft-minded person would have pitied them.'

'Were there a great number of people removed at that time?'

'I cannot give the number but yon was the first removal in the strath.'

'Who got the place after the people were removed?'

'Sellar got it, but in five years time we had a second removal.'

'Who got the place from which you were removed the second time?'

'I believe Sellar. I was in Caithness herding at the time but I suppose it was just Sellar who got it.'

Betsag turned as she stood by the fire, prodding the potatoes in the pot with a fork to discover whether they were cooked. 'That will be the big sheep farmhouse he built at the mouth of the strath,' she interrupted, 'the one Captain Hunter had till he sold it. Aye, there was many a curse put on the old owner of that house.'

'The people should have risen against him,' said Christine.

'What could they do?' asked Tom. 'They tried to bring him to justice, and he was acquitted of his crimes by a jury in Inverness. Shall I read you any more?'

'Yes, do go on,' Christine urged him. So Tom adopted the voice of the Commissioner again, resuming his questions.

'You stated that your father and mother and the family went away with the stock of cows and horses in the morning, and that they left you and your brother in the house lying asleep in the bed.'

'Yes.'

'How do you explain that your father and mother left their two sons alone in the house in bed asleep when they went away themselves.'

'Because we were weak and young and they were sure we would sleep to nine or ten o'clock, when they would be back again. My father was back before I was ten minutes out of the river.'

'How far had your father to go? How far was the new place from the old?'

'About a mile and a half, to a place which was an unculti-vated piece of ground until then.'

'What sort of a place was it? Was it worse than the old place?'

'It was a place that never was laboured before.'

'Was he assisted to build his house?'

'No, he had to build his house with feal, and no stone at all.'

'Did the proprietor give him any stones to build a new house?'

'No.'

'Did he give him any compensation for the old house he left?'

'Nothing in the world.'

'How long was he in this new place?'

'Five years, when he got his second removal.'

'Why did he get the second removal?'

'To the Point, to the worst place there is in the district.' Tom put down the book, saying, 'That was a question he didn't understand properly, but it didn't matter. Wasn't it cunning of Sellar to keep putting people on the uncultivated ground, and then moving them on again once they had dug and drained it?'

He saw his wife take up the two black pots, the one above the fire, the other on the ledge beside it, and carry them to the little room built on the back of the house behind the kitchen, with a lean-to roof.

'Christine comes all this way to see us,' he recalled, 'and you give her nothing to eat.'

'How can I?' retorted Betsag from the back, 'with your fiddling and your recitations?' She was removing the lump of meat that had been cooking in the broth. Then she put a pile of potatoes from the other pot on a plate, with which she returned to place it in the centre of the table. Next she surrounded this with three steaming plates of soup, filled with barley and scraps of vegetable and the goodness of the meat.

'Sit in now,' said Betsag. 'You say a grace, Tom.'

Geordie rose silently from beside the fire and joined his brother and Christine at the table while Betsag returned to the back room. Tom placed a hand over his brow and delivered his grace in a scarcely audible whisper. Then each of them placed a potato in their broth: and whether it was the effect of the grace or of the savoury smell that rose with the steam from their plates, the atmosphere of gloom which had filled the room with memories of the evictions vanished. So did the soup, which Betsag replaced with slices of meat to which more potatoes were added from the plate in the centre of the table until she must replenish it. At last Betsag made the tea, leaving the pot to simmer beside the fire while she brought scones and bread, cheese and jam.

'I couldn't take another cup,' Christine protested, as her aunt came to her with the teapot a second time. 'I'm full.'

'If it was salt herring you were eating you would have drunk another cup,' laughed Tom, 'and then you would be glooging at the dance.'

'If my father will let me go to it,' said Christine, and Betsag drew in her breath sympathetically while Tom shook his head in mock censure.

Early in the afternoon Christine said goodbye to Betsag and Tom's silent brother, and set off with her uncle on the windy road to meet the bus. The gale had increased if anything, so that they could hardly speak to one another as they leant against its gusts. When they reached the coast road beside the inn they had to wait there as Christine had seen the shawled figures waiting on her outward journey. The bus kept to no timetable as it trundled home from the east, delivering messages and collecting passengers.

Tom looked over his shoulder at the inn more than once, and every time he did so Christine stared more anxiously for the bus to come climbing the hill, round the bend.

'You go home, Tom,' she said finally. 'There's no sense in you standing out here in the cold.'

'It's you I'm worried about,' her uncle replied. 'You'll be starved in that bus. Come inside while we're waiting and we'll give you something to warm you up.'

'Oh, I've never tasted,' protested Christine, which was not quite true. She had once taken the tiniest sip. 'But you go in, and I'll just wait here in case the bus comes.'

Off went Tom while Christine, holding the knot of her scarf under her chin, continued to scan the fifty yards of road that ran round the corner of the dyke. There was nobody else waiting to catch the bus. Suppose it had passed already. She had begun to shiver by the time Tom returned. One of his hands was in the pocket of the coat he was wearing, and when he withdrew it Christine saw that it contained a glass of whisky.

'Here, take this,' he said. 'It will warm you on your journey.'

Christine knew it was true, and she also knew how deeply her father would disapprove, and because she had spent so much of her life resisting her father's taboos, this added to its attraction in her eyes.

'Come,' coaxed Tom. 'You will hardly notice the cold when you have taken it.'

'But my father will get the smell of it when I go home.'

'Then it will do good to the two of you,' said Tom. 'Och eeon, it is a powerful medicine.'

Christine looked down the road again. The bus might come at any moment and here she was, arguing over a glass of whisky with her uncle in the road. There was only one thing for it. She took the glass without another word, flung her head back, and poured the entire contents down her throat in one fiery gulp. She spluttered and shuddered as she handed the glass back to Tom, but not a word could she say. He had hardly replaced it in his pocket when the bus appeared round the bend and wheezed to a stop by the dyke opposite. She took Tom's hand and shook it effusively.

'Well, cheerio and thank you,' she said, and floated across the road.

The bus was exceptionally full and contained a high proportion of young people, evidently coming to the dance. Near the front, in one of the seats behind the driver, sat the Minister. Perhaps out of respect for the cloth, the place beside him was empty. Christine smiled to everyone as she came aboard and looked everywhere behind the Minister for a vacant seat, while the driver engaged bottom gear to resume his uphill journey. But she could not see one, and the Minister moved over slightly, inviting her to join him. There was nothing for it but to do so.

She tried to hold her breath. The Minister was a frequent visitor to her home and she knew his views on drink. On the other hand, he did not condemn smoking as sinful, in fact he smoked himself and was doing so now. Christine's dislike of the smell of tobacco amounted almost to an allergy, so that she held her breath partly because she was afraid it would make her sick. But soon she was forced to let it out in a great gust, and then the Minister turned on her a look of horror and amazement. The bus lurched and swayed on the uneven road and the noise of its engine reverberated in her ears. She took a deep breath and the smoke from the Minister's cigarette made her feel dizzy, or perhaps it was the whisky. At least the Minister did not address her, but sat with pursed lips, except when he drew on his cigarette.

The day had been dark, and the night fell early and black. Because of the black-out regulations there were no lights inside the bus, only the dimmed headlights on the road ahead. But Christine found herself back at home where a golden ray shone from the tea-tray and lit the harmonium. From this instrument, although nobody was playing it, came the slow notes of a penitential psalm. She saw the little wicker table with its cloth of light green imitation silk, and on it the great black Bible. The heavenly light from the tea-tray fell on the Bible also. Her father was beside it, pronouncing judgment in sorrowful accents on the whole family at the Point. Betsag stood before him, with coffin-nails for teeth, while Tom crouched beside his coffin and his witless brother sat tapping his foot as the smoke bellowed out beside him in great balloons. The smell of the smoke was dreadful.

'The sins of the fathers shall be visited on their children unto the third and fourth generation,' declared her father between pursed lips. There they were, the terrified child trying to ford the river with his baby brother on his back while houses burned in the distance. Her father turned to her. Had she not danced in her heart while the devil fiddled, and drunk the cup of iniquity?

'I can smell it on your breath,' he said, and the Minister turned to nod in agreement, blowing sulphurous fumes in her face.

Christine woke with a start as bursts of rain suddenly hit the windows of the bus with a slap. In front of her the driver was crouched over his wheel, scanning the road in the dim headlights as it twisted through the desolate countryside. She felt a warm glow inside her and a vast sense of relief that the real world held none of the terrors of her dream. She clung to the happy memory of her visit to Tom's home on the Point until she found herself back there, telling Betsag about the matron of her hospital in Inverness. It was so warm and companionable among the people whom God had not chosen. The storm boomed in the kitchen chimney but within there was understanding and merriment. Nurse Barbara was there, stroking a cat in her lap.

'I like this cat like one of my own bairns,' she said. 'It is so near me.' She said it in Gaelic and Christine could understand her.

Then Tom struck up a tune on his fiddle, and a man walked through the door and Tom stopped and pointed his bow at him and said, 'that's Patrick Sellar, the wicked factor.'

'No it's not,' Christine told him. 'You only think that because he lives in Sellar's house. It's Donald.' So then Tom began to play again and she and Donald danced, and her father said, 'you will be damned.'

But she no longer cared, either sleeping or waking, as she realized when she joined the general exodus at her village and considered her experiences on her short walk home.

On the same stormy afternoon, Donald was travelling north on another bus from the nearest railhead. He could see nothing from its windows on his journey from the station, but he had travelled along the strath so often that he knew every inch of the road by heart. He could picture the tufted rocks where the Owen Malloch flowed into the river and the sward of Dunvedan, though he did not know what Patrick Sellar had done there so long ago. A swing to the left, a short climb uphill, and he recalled the little wood of stunted birches, the delta of stones scattered down the hillside by a flood. Beyond fields in a twist of the river lay his former home, but though he strained his eyes at the window he could hardly make out its silhouette in the blackness.

Would Angus be expecting him? He alighted in the village, the only passenger to do so, and set off almost furtively before anyone coming to meet the bus could accost him. There would be time later to resume old acquaintances, once he had adjusted his mind to the strange circumstances of his homecoming. After a moment's hesitation he decided it would be unwise to attempt the short cut to the other side of the bay on such a night as this, so he walked down the road between the cliffs and the glebe fields until he reached the gravel path that ran out to the headland. It was now that the wind really caught him, swinging his suitcase out and tearing at the mackintosh he was wearing over a civilian suit. Donald moved slowly, concentrating on his surroundings with every faculty he possessed of touch and sight and sound.

Fortunately for him, the blackout regulations were not being rigorously observed. As Donald left the path to climb the brae behind the football field he saw a tiny point of light at the house in which Jackie had gone to live after his marriage, and a less tiny gleam on the slope above it where Angus and the his mother lived.

The house seemed strangely small to Donald as he entered, and Jean seemed small.

'Come away in, Donnie,' she called. 'It's good to see you. Is Angie not with you? He was down to meet the bus.'

'Oh I'm sorry,' said Donald guiltily. 'I didn't wait to look.'

'Och never mind,' Jean reassured him. 'It's that dark out. He was maybe in one of the houses when the bus came. Here, take off your coat and sit in to the fire. Will you never stop growing? They must feed you well in the army. I'll take your bag.'

'Thank you very much for letting me come to stay like this,' said Donald as he shed his bag and coat and grew accustomed to the warmth and light.

'Be quiet,' Jean replied. 'We're that pleased to see you again.' She inspected him with a smile, then added, 'you're going the English very good.'

She nodded to the chair with rexine armrests, newly repaired but otherwise the same as when Magnus had sat there. Embarrassed to be occupying his seat as well as by Jean's remark, Donald nevertheless went and sat in it.

'Christine told me that Neil and Jack are away at the war,' he said. 'Have you had news of them?'

'Neil will be at sea somewhere,' Jean replied. 'He was with the Navy at Dunkirk. He is a Leading Seaman now.' She went to the press and fetched a photograph to show Donald. Neil was grinning characteristically in his naval uniform, but he looked much older than Donald remembered him.

'And what about Jack?'

'He was taken a prisoner in France.'

'Oh, I'm sorry,' Donald muttered. Why had Christine not told him.

'We'll manage all right with Angus at home,' Jean went on quickly. 'He can see to everything. As long as he stays.'

'They can't call him up,' Donald tried to reassure her, 'not when he's in agriculture.'

'But there's nothing to stop him going of his own accord. He's nineteen like yourself, and he may want to go.' The conversation ended abruptly as Angus himself came in through the door.

'Hullo, Donnie,' he said, shaking him heartily by the hand. 'So you reached. It's grand to see you back here.' The two youths eyed each other in the searching way that strangers do when they feel certain that they have met somewhere before. Angus looked rather like Neil, as Donald remembered him. He was short and thick-set. Donald was now far taller, and just as Jean had remarked on his English accent, so he was now more aware of Angie's speech, the rich inflections of one who had never left the Highlands.

'I'm sorry I didn't wait for you at the bus,' Donald apologized. 'It was very good of you to meet it, especially on a night like this.'

'That's all right,' said Angus. 'I saw Christine off the bus anyway.'

He turned to his mother. 'She went to the Point, never mind what her father said. The row that will be in it now she has reached home!' Angus adopted Neil's look, expressive of signs and wonders.

'How?' asked her mother.

'She had taken drink,' Angus disclosed in an awful voice.

'But she wasn't on the bus,' Donald objected, out of touch with Angus' humour.

'It was the coast bus she was on, from the Point,' Angus turned to explain to him.

'But surely Christine doesn't drink,' Donald floundered on, and his shocked expression was too much for Angus.

'She just made the house of it, and up the stairs to her bed,' he pronounced in a sepulchral voice. His mother glanced quickly from one to the other and cut the conversation short.

'Sit in to your tea, the two of you or you will never be at the dance,' she said. While they were eating, she asked Donald about his parents down near Inverness, and then Angus asked him all about his life in the army.

Talking about his war service, Donald tried to feel as adult as Angus sounded, who had only been looking after a croft here while he had been a prefect at his school. Angus plied him with

91

questions so eagerly, showed so much respect, envy almost, that Donald felt a surge of self-confidence. When he left the kitchen after tea to take his bag up to his room, Jean turned to her son.

'Had Christine really been drinking?' she asked.

'Not at all,' Angus laughed. 'Just that she was shivering, waiting for the bus at the Point Inn, so Tom made her take a dram to warm her up. She told me she was afraid they would smell it on her breath when she reached home.'

'Aye, they're gey narrow,' sighed Jean.

Donald returned and they resumed their talk, seated either side of the fire, until Angus rose and went to the back to put on his coat.

'I'll fetch Christine,' he said. 'She'll maybe not get out of the house without assistance.'

'Shall I come?' asked Donald.

'We'll see you at the dance,' Angus replied, laying one hand flat on the torch that sat on the press. 'Be sure you don't go without this in your pocket.' Then he was gone.

Donald's sense of well-being vanished. It hadn't occurred to him that Angus would be taking Christine to the dance, but then Christine hadn't told him there would be a dance on the night of his arrival. Perhaps she didn't know herself until she arrived home. Of course, she and Angus had been at school together, seeing one another all the time since his parents had moved to Inverness. Donald realized that at tea Angus had been asking all the questions, encouraging him to talk about himself. But what was there for him to ask Angus, who had never left the district? Plenty, now he came to think of it. He sat gazing moodily into the fire while Jean washed the dishes in the scullery at the back.

'You're the quiet one,' she called out to him. Donald roused himself.

'I'll go and change into my uniform,' he said. 'We're not supposed to wear civilian clothes and I'd better not risk it in a public place.' Although he had brought his battledress as a precaution, he had not had the slightest intention of putting it on until this moment.

Upstairs there were two bedrooms, with skylights in the zinc roof, on which the wind beat loudly. Angus had one of these rooms and Donald was given the other. Jean slept in the closet room downstairs in which Magnus had lain when he was ill. Donald dressed in his uniform with great care, gave his shoes a rub, and returned to the kitchen.

'You do look smart,' Jean exclaimed. 'All the girls will be after you.' But Donald was not thinking of all the girls: he was thinking about Christine. He ought to have jumped at the invitation to stay in her home, except that perhaps her parents might have forbidden him to take her to the dance. Supposing that had happened, and then Angus had arrived and taken her instead, the situation might have been worse. Donald was so preoccupied by these thoughts that he would have left the house without the torch if Jean had not reminded him. He took the short cut across the sands this time, and saw the white crests of the waves breaking on the beach with a roar in the surrounding blackness. He wondered whether Neil could be out on such a sea and shivered.

Before the war, a dance would never have become lively in the village hall until sometime between nine and ten o'clock, but now people were making an earlier start. When Donald looked in there were several couples prancing round to the strains of a Scottische played on the accordion, and most of them were elderly enough to look much the same as Donald remembered them. But there were some unfamiliar faces, perhaps of people who had come in from distant villages. Angus and Christine were not there, so after Donald had paid his entrance fee and exchanged a few words with those who greeted him, he walked out to where a group was standing in conversation by the door.

The hall was constructed of wood painted yellow, and it had a red corrugated iron roof. The windows had been boarded up, so that there was ventilation only when the door opened to throw an unpatriotic light on the group in the road beyond it. These welcomed Donald affably, and with only a touch of formality drew him into their talk. Soon they were questioning him about the army and his life in the south. The wind had dropped, and anyway they were gathered on the lea side of the hall, but the day's storm had moulded their shapes, the hunched shoulders, hands in pockets.

So flattering were their attentions to Donald that he quite forgot Christine until it suddenly occurred to him that she and Angus might have walked past into the hall without his noticing. The music had stopped. He excused himself, left his companions and went back through the door. All the girls were sitting along the benches down one side of the hall, all the men on the other, some sitting, some standing. Blinking in the bright light, Donald peered at the row of girls without finding Christine among them. Observing him there in uniform near the entrance, some of the girls turned smiling to one another, obviously discussing him. Although he thought he recognized some of their features, he could not be sure who any of them were although he told himself that he must have known most of them when they were young and it was clear that they recognized him. He watched them whispering to one another with an occasional glance in his direction and wilted with embarrassment. He wished he had not dressed in his army uniform. Where were Christine and Angus?

'Take your partners for Strip the Willow,' someone called out, and from the two sides of the hall people trailed out to form two lines facing one another. A girl or two glanced at Donald expectantly. All he had to do was to join the line of men at any point. He was about to take the plunge when the thought struck him. Christine must have gone drinking again. He swivelled round on his heels, pushed open the hall door, and cast a long shadow in the shaft of light before it closed again.

'Who's coming for a drink?' he called to a group still standing out in the darkness. Three or four figures, he could not tell who they were until they spoke, moved forward and accompanied him up the road. Their companionship revived his spirits a little.

The older village inns on the north coast stand at the distances from one another at which horses had to be changed in the days of coaches. The one Donald was heading for was the next hostelry to the west after the Point Inn, and it stood near the summit of the road before this descended to the river mouth and his former home. He had never entered its bar before, but then he had not visited any pub before he joined the army. He was surprised that it was so small, nothing more than a long narrow corridor of wood, with the counter running its entire length along one side.

It contained half a dozen drinkers, all of them men, and Donald realized at once that neither Christine nor any other girl would enter here. He insisted on buying the first round, and since there were four of them, he ordered that number of large whiskies. The bar became more crowded, the air thick with tobacco smoke. But the atmosphere was warm and friendly, and Donald relaxed into a mood of confidence and ease such as he had not experienced since his arrival. Despite the strange circumstances of his return, he now felt as though he had come home. After the third round he told his companions that he would walk back to the hall to discover whether Angus had arrived there. If not, he would return. He did not mention Christine.

'Donnie's just the same,' one of them remarked after he had left.

'Except he's lost the burr in his speech,' said another.

'He talks like a toff now, but he doesn't act like one.'

'His father behaved like one without talking like it.'

'Funny that Donnie isn't an officer.'

'Why?'

'Well his father is, or was.'

'But now there's a war on.' They laughed and changed the subject.

The hall was thick with dancers by the time Donald reached it again, twirling in a waltz to the air of the song in praise of Islay. Donald did not remain standing by the door this time, but edged his way down the side of the hall, inspecting the couples. Once or twice he moved far enough from the wall for a couple to dance round the outside of him. Then he saw Angus waltzing with Christine, but they were too occupied with one another to notice him, and soon they had vanished among the other dancers. Donald stood where he was until they came round again, but they passed him by without taking their eyes off one another. Donald jostled his way back to the door and returned to the bar. It was only after the dance, when Christine had gone to join the other girls on their bench, that someone mentioned to Angus that Donald looked in.

'I think he's hitting the bottle,' his informant added. So Angus was not taken completely unawares when Donald returned after the bar had closed.

There were four sets of the eightsome reel in progress, and Donald planted himself just outside the circle in which Angus and Christine were dancing. He stared without concentrating, and when Christine smiled at him on her way past he did not respond.

'Hullo, Donnie,' Angus called to him heartily when the reel was over, 'so you turned up.' Donald ignored him and made for Christine as she strolled to the benches opposite.

'Why won't you dance with me?' he asked.

'But you only just came,' she replied, giving him an open, amused look.

'Then let's dance now.'

'But the dance is finished,' said Christine and, observing his condition, and how so many people in the hall were watching them, she tried to move away to where the other girls were sitting. But Donald caught her by the arm.

'Let go of me,' she protested, and when he still clutched her she added, 'you're drunk.'

'Me drunk,' Donald laughed. 'You're a fine one to talk about anyone being drunk.'

At this point he let Christine go as Angus took him with one arm firmly round his waist and pulled him down the hall, saying, 'You're getting out of here.' The floor of the hall was now empty, the dancers lined along the walls as Angus forced Donald towards the door. But before they reached it, Donald struggled free and turned to face him.

'You take your hands off me,' he threatened. 'If you want to fight, why don't you join up, you shirker?' At that, Christine called hysterically,

'Get out of here. Go back where you belong.'

The words were accompanied by a blow from Angus that caught him on the jaw and toppled him off his uncertain balance. Christine came running across.

'I'm sorry,' Angus said to her. 'But don't worry. I'll take Donnie back home. Look, he's broken the torch.' And Angus picked up the torch that Donald had been grasping all this time, its glass shattered in the fall. Christine rushed from the hall before anyone could witness her tears, and sped home.

Angus helped Donald up from the floor while others came forward to lend a hand.

'I'll manage, thanks,' Donald mumbled to those who tried to help. He allowed Angus to propel him through the door, but as soon as they were outside he protested.

'I can walk on my own.'

'Then keep by me. We'll take the short cut.'

'I'm sorry,' said Donald.

'Forget it,' said Angus.

The wind had veered through 180 degrees in the capricious manner of the weather along this coast. Now it was no more than a mild breeze, while the clouds above were mere tatters through which the moon came and went. In the clear atmosphere the floor of heaven appeared to be paved with diamonds. The two youths reached the bay in silence, to find the wet sands from which the tide had receded glistening in an eerie light.

'You walk ahead and I'll follow,' said Angus, as though recalling the day when they had scrambled as children on the headland opposite. Donald chose the firm sand just below the high tide mark and Angus followed his meandering footprints until suddenly he stopped and was sick. Then Angus caught up with him and held him with clumsy concern as he retched. For a moment, after he had finished, Donald clung to Angus as a drowning man might, then they resumed their trudge across the bay, two ghosts in a lost world. Over the horizon to the north the Merry Dancers appeared, their green and white fingers moving in stately procession.

'Look, the northern lights,' called Angus, but Donald did not look up. His mind had cleared when he was sick and his friend's earlier words had transported him back in time. He was experiencing the greatest grief, looking back through his misery at a time of happiness. They climbed the brae until the island came in sight, a dark hump ringed with white surf by the still tempestuous ocean. Donald turned to look at it. He would never visit that island now.

At last they reached the house, and Angus took Donald in by the front door, which was rarely used but never locked, and straight up the stairs to his room.

'I'll leave in the morning,' said Donald.

'You've no need to do that.'

'Thanks very much, but I must.

'Then I'll tell Mam. Have a good sleep, Donnie, and you'll feel fine.'

Jean must have heard them come in and go upstairs, but when Angus entered the kitchen she only said, 'You're back early.'

'Donnie has to leave in the morning,that's why,' Angus answered, and sat down beside his mother on the couch to the right of the fire. For a long time he sat there in silence, staring at the floor, while she refrained from questioning him. But perhaps she realized that he might never speak unless she invited him to, because finally she asked,

'Whatever's the matter with you, lad?'

'Mam, I've something to tell you.'

'Well, what is it?'

'It is that I'll need to leave too, to join the army.'

'But you're needed here.'

'I know. I'm sorry. But there will be others to help, and it's the same all over.' He gave his mother an imploring look that stopped her as she was about to speak. She rose and walked across to the door of her bedroom.

'You will have to do as you think right,' she said without turning. 'Good night, Angus,' and then the door closed behind her.

6

The news which reached Donald's parents after he had returned to his unit a week later came as a shock to Captain
Hunter. His son had been refused a commission in his regiment. He soothed his sense of humiliation by railing against the
new democratic methods of promotion, and wrote to Sir
William Jones, asking whether anything could be done to
rectify the injustice in the interests of the war effort.

As soon as Sir William's public duties permitted, he sent his
commiserations to the Hunters on Donald's misfortune. He
had known Donald all his life, he dictated to his secretary as
though he were giving a testimonial, and he was convinced
that his godson possessed all the qualities of an officer. Had he
not been a prefect at Stellmore? Sir William went on to tell
Captain Hunter about the newly formed Intelligence Corps,
adding discreetly that Hunter might not approve of this new-
fangled body, might prefer the old method of seconding officers
from their regiments for intelligence duties. This would still
continue, but the new Corps could now recruit others by direct
commission into its ranks. Of course there was a danger that
they were creating a corps of bolshies – only time would tell –
but at least this organization would offer openings to people of
a high standard of education. Sir William promised to talk to
somebody who would talk to someone else.

While Captain Hunter was torn by conflicting feelings from
the moment he read these words, and Donald's name passed
from ear to influential ear in distant offices, he was resuming
his life at a camp in the south of England, filled with a misery
that had nothing to do with whether he held a commission or
not. It was so inward-looking that none of the unhappiness he
had brought to others intruded on it. He gave no thought to
whether he had disappointed his father. He knew nothing of

the feelings of Angie's mother, threatened with the loss of her last remaining son.

Donald's camp lay close to an ancient and prosperous provincial town, its entrance leading to a road that ran to the town centre. For a short distance this road was lined by trim council houses, then by other semi-detached houses in patterned brick and applied half-timbering. Beyond these it twisted round a stone assembly hall and passed between houses of an age before town-planning was thought of, until it reached the High Street. Donald knew every inch of this road. He had stamped down it in iron-studded boots and in walking-out shoes. He had ambled along it on fine days and hustled through it in the rain. He had whistled down it sober, and since his return from leave he had more frequently sung his way up it in jostling parties, drunk.

As he walked down it on this evening, alone and lonely, the blacked-out houses represented to him a cold and hostile world. The fact that so many people were suffering the horrors of the Blitz, that the approaching year of 1941 might bring his country to defeat and ruin, these were woes less real to him than the despair within. As Donald passed along the street, he wished he had remained in the canteen amongst all the clatter and the banter. But that had become intolerable too. The familiarity of strangers in a confined space somehow reminded him that he belonged nowhere.

'You're a dark horse, Jock,' one of them had said to him in the canteen, not meaning any harm. Of course he was. The rest of them had the jokes of a common background to share, they could boast of the girls they had seduced, discuss their families. Could he tell them how he had overcome his aversion to cricket at school and become a prefect, or let them into the secret of the island he had never visited?

Donald made an effort to see himself from outside himself, to pretend he was one of these darkened windows with the tiny slits of light round the edges, watching him pass. He listened to the footfall and saw the figure, six foot in khaki, the dark horse. It possessed an army number, different from anyone else's, but it wore the same uniform, obeyed the same orders, lived in the same stables. To be a real person like his companions, rather than a dark horse, he must possess more than just a separate number to identify him. He must have a country and be one of its inhabitants.

His thoughts returned to the north coast, until he deliberately shut his mind against the memory of his recent visit. How could he ever go back there? He turned to the picture of his parents, but this raised the spectre of his father's reaction when he learned that Donald had been refused a commission. His mother had written sympathetically while his father had sent no message. Donald could easily imagine why. He tried to take comfort in the warmth and approval of the Joneses. Would Lady Jones regard him with the same affection when she heard he was to remain in the ranks?

'My dear, he's gone all rustic again,' he could almost hear her saying to Lady Charterford with an apologetic laugh. Anyway, he realized, her world would never be his, whatever his rank.

He had reached the High Street. It was much broader than the twisting road he had left, and ran straight through the centre of the old town. He came to the cinema and stood aimlessly, by force of habit, looking at the still photographs in its dim porch. A familiar film actress stood, partially dressed, in a bedroom, menaced by a famous film actor. In how many varieties of plot had they met like this? Another picture showed the same actor lurking at a street corner in the rain, his pistol at the ready. There was a kissing scene and a death scene. Presently there was also someone else studying these pictures.

'D'you think it's worth seeing?' she turned and asked Donald.

'It looks awful to me,' he replied, taking as close a look at her as he could in such a light. She was young and fluffy, and somehow he didn't feel at all embarrassed, sharing this porch with her, although he felt sure he had never seen her before.

'That's what I think,' she agreed. 'Oh well, I'll just go back home. Are you from the camp?'

'How did you guess?' They both laughed.

'D'you like it here?' she asked. 'I mean, d'you know a lot of people here?'

'I don't know a soul outside the camp.'

'Oh we're a stuffy lot in this town,' she confessed. 'But I'll show you I'm not by letting you walk back with me to where I live. Now don't say no. I may need protection with all you soldiers roaming around in the dark.'

Donald's immediate thought was that he was being picked up, but this had never happened to him before and he couldn't be certain. He had very little money on him, if that was what she was after. But her manner seemed open and innocent enough, and when Donald turned to her again her smile was frank and simple.

'I certainly won't say no,' he replied, feeling a great deal more light-hearted already. 'I'd like very much to walk back with you.' He really meant it, and it sounded as though he did.

'What's your name?' she asked him as they strolled along the dark High Street.

'Donald.' He wasn't sure whether he had stopped at that as a precaution or because it was right in the circumstances. It seemed acceptable enough.

'I'm Estelle.'

'That's an unusual name.'

'Oh yes, it's a very uncommon name.' Estelle sounded immensely pleased by Donald's observation. 'Some names are so common,' she added, and took his arm. 'Now you must tell me all about yourself. Where do you come from?'

'Scotland.'

'You don't sound like it.' There was a note of reproof in Estelle's reply, as though she suspected him of trying to hoodwink her. How could he prove it? He couldn't show her his paybook out here in the dark.

'Well, they call me Jock at the camp,' he said aggressively enough for her to give his arm a squeeze and say soothingly,

'All right, I believe you. It's just that you sound, well, so refined.' She was beginning to speak in a more refined accent herself.

'Of course you'll be an officer soon, won't you Don?' She gave his arm another squeeze, as though she were already intimate with an officer.

'No I shan't be an officer,' he replied decisively. She was trying to turn him into someone he was not. 'Haven't you heard that the best English is spoken in Inverness? That's where I come from.' He felt suddenly confident and elated, and was delighted to discover that Estelle was impressed.

'It sounds lovely, the way you speak,' she purred. 'Do you ever wear kilts?' Donald winced at the term.

'Hardly, in the Essex Regiment,' he replied, and they both

102

laughed.

Without turning off the High Street, they had reached the terraces of undetached houses on the edge of the town. Each possessed two floors and a little plot of garden in front. Estelle put her hand on the wooden gate that gave entrance to one of these and said, 'Well, here we are.'

Donald's elation vanished. 'Oh dear,' he said. He had felt happy, arm in arm with this artless girl who asked him questions and showed she liked him.

'We must meet again,' he said hurriedly. 'We can meet in the town. Let's see when I'll be off next.' Estelle just stood and giggled, her hand on the gate.

'Don't be silly,' she said. 'Come in and have something to eat. The night's young.' Donald realized he had never asked Estelle anything about herself. He couldn't even tell how old she was. Eighteen, he guessed. Would he have to spend the evening talking to her parents? Would they mind Estelle bringing him home like this? It was too late to start worrying about such things now.

'Thanks very much, Estelle,' he said. She seemed anxious not to linger in the road, talking, as she hurried forward to the door, groping in her bag. From it she took a key, unlocked the door, and hustled Donald through it. She pushed it shut behind her, leaving them standing in the hall in total darkness. The next instant Donald felt Estelle's fluffy hair against his cheek and she was kissing him on the lips. Although he was nineteen years of age, it was the first time he had kissed a girl like this, her tongue exploring the gap between his teeth.

But she broke away just as he was beginning to respond, as though bashful over what had occurred, and fluttered off to the living room where she switched on the light. Donald followed her.

'Take your coat off and make yourself comfortable,' she said, kneeling to put coal on the sunken fire.

'Here, let me do that.' But she was already finished and away out of the room.

It was a small one, the bow window covered by black-out curtains. Its suite of two armchairs and a sofa was very new-looking, and there was an unframed mirror hanging from chains above the fireplace. The mantelpiece was of green glazed tiles, and there was a framed photograph on it which

103

immediately caught Donald's eye. Estelle was standing arm-in-arm with a sergeant in uniform whose size dwarfed her. She was smiling demurely while he stared stolidly over a thin black moustache. He did not look old enough to be her father, neither was there any family resemblance to suggest that he might be her brother.

Donald removed his greatcoat and flung it over the back of one of the chairs. Then, because the portrait on the mantelpiece made him feel uneasy, he sat back on the sofa, his army boots stretched out to the fire, in a rather exaggerated pose of relaxation. It must be all right whoever the sergeant was, he told himself, otherwise Estelle would not have invited him in. He hadn't forced himself on her, far from it. But perhaps he ought to have asked her a few questions on the way here. It was all the fault of his upbringing, he reflected. He had been taught that it was rude to ask personal questions, and this was the result. Yet the mystery contributed to his feeling of exhilaration.

He could not fathom how Estelle came to have the run of this place all to herself. Her parents could hardly have gone to bed yet. Perhaps they were out paying a visit. Anyway, here he was, the guest of a pretty girl who had invited him home. The fire blazed up, and Donald undid the buttons of his tunic and sank more comfortably into the rather hard small sofa, remembering her kiss. His attitude was no longer a pose.

Estelle came back, carrying a tray of tea and little cakes, and kicked the door shut behind her. She placed the tray on a low square table by Donald's right elbow, then subsided into the sofa on his left.

'Who's that in the photo with you?' he asked.

'Guess,' replied Estelle, giving her artless giggle. She lent across him to pour the tea beyond with her left hand, and it was only then that he noticed.

'You're married,' he said, and a funny feeling ran down his spine. But he couldn't move because she was leaning heavily on him, pouring tea into a cup. He could feel the vibration in his lap as she still giggled.

'Right first time.' Donald could see the photograph above her hair. He could not assess her husband's features from this distance, only his size in the sergeant's uniform.

'When is he coming?' Donald asked as calmly as he could.

'What'll he say?'

'Who? George?' Estelle had finished pouring the tea and eased herself slowly back from Donald's lap. There was innocent amusement in her pert little face.

'Don't worry, Don. He won't be back till the weekend.' She glanced up at the photograph herself and explained, 'He's in the Sappers. He doesn't get home all that often, and he always lets me know in advance.' She gave Donald a glance that he was too preoccupied to notice, let alone interpret. Then she resorted to the method of communication she had already used in the darkness of the hall.

At first Donald's response was lukewarm, as he considered that Sergeant George would be coming home at the weekend and today was Thursday. Then the old adage came to mind, that a miss is as good as a mile. Meanwhile, Estelle held the trump card for anyone as sexually inexperienced as Donald, and he soon succumbed to it. His reservations were swept away by a surge of many sensations, the tickle of fluffy hair on his cheek, the weight so expertly deployed in his lap, the scent in his nostrils, and the wide hungry lips. Donald responded with an ardour that drew from Estelle a surprised, ecstatic sigh.

Behind Donald's closed eyes there floated the image of Christine, calling him a drunkard in front of everyone at the dance, Angus hitting him by the door. The nightmare of the past dissolved in the bliss of the present. Estelle sighed again as Donald's arms tightened around her.

'Heavens,' she exclaimed, breaking free, 'are you Scots all like that? You act so mild the rest of the time.'

Suddenly there was a loud knock at the front door. Donald leapt to his feet. He stood there staring at Estelle, waiting for her to say something. But she put a finger to her lips, made silently for the tea tray, poured the tea from the two cups back into the pot, and picked up the tray.

'Quick,' she whispered, 'get your cap and coat and go out the back. Don't make a sound.' She nodded to him to open the door when he was ready, and they both tiptoed down the dark passage to the kitchen behind the stairs, muffled by the noise of renewed knocking. Estelle unlocked the back door, and locked it again behind him without the exchange of another word.

Beyond the kitchen door there was an invisible step that nearly pitched Donald headlong. As he stumbled forward blindly, his boot hit metal with a bang and his body met something round and hard. A dustbin. Donald was negotiating his way round this cautiously, at the same time as he tried to don his greatcoat without losing his cap, when a voice boomed from the darkness behind him. He ducked behind the dustbin just as the back door was flung open, sending an illegal shaft of light down the area.

'Come in, you,' the voice threatened. Donald felt his heart thump faster and faster as he crouched there, fumbling the buttons of his battledress jacket with terror-stricken fingers.

'Come on, blast you. I know you're out there, so you might just as well come in.'

'Oh stop being so silly,' came the voice of Estelle. 'You'll have me in prison, showing a light like this. come in and shut the door.' And to Donald's astonishment, the owner of the booming voice did exactly as he was told. Half paralysed with fear still, he stood up again. He tried to concentrate, believing that a single detail overlooked might be fatal. He finished buttoning his jacket, did up all the buttons of his greatcoat, and placed his forage cap on his head. He tiptoed cautiously away from the house, hoping he would find a back gate.

The kitchen door opened again, revealing the exit in a beam of light. It was a door in a high wall. Suppose it was locked. Donald stood transfixed in the beam, and as fear stabbed him again he forced himself to look round. Estelle was standing alone in the doorway. Then she closed the door and trotted down the area towards him.

'Wasn't that a lark?' she whispered to him between giggles as she took his arm. 'Me thinking it was George. Course I ought to have known he never comes except when he says.' What a fool, thought Donald, as Estelle held him closer, shaking with mirth.

'Wasn't it George?'

'No.' She raised her face to him, lips open, and as fear fell away from him Donald responded, and they swayed together in the dark. Their hushed, conspiratorial laughter came in little gusts. Estelle's husband was not in the house after all. Then Donald pushed her from him.

'But if it wasn't George, who was it?' he asked.

'Bert.' She went on laughing, her head snuggling into Donald's greatcoat.

'But who's Bert?'

'Don't you know? You ought to. He's from your camp.' Donald disentangled himself from Estelle a second time.

'What's his other name?'

'Oh I don't know. He's just Bert.' She tried not to let Donald go. 'He's not there any more,' she told him. 'I made him leave after all that fuss. I said I wasn't having that kind of carry-on in my house. You should have seen me pretending I was angry.' She began to giggle again. 'You can come back inside now. Bert's gone.'

But by now she had lost Donald as well. He saw himself as just anyone in khaki, looking at the pictures outside the cinema, nobody special whom she had taken a fancy to, not even a Scot or a potential officer, let alone the individual called Donald Hunter. Others just knocked on Estelle's door when they felt like it, and he had scuttled out to make room for the next.

'You should have let Bert stay,' he told her.

'Oh don't talk like that, Don,' she pleaded. 'I'm sorry, really I am. I couldn't help it.' Donald was beginning to edge away towards the back door, and she spoke faster. 'I'll tell you what. I promise I'll break off with Bert. Then I can go with you regular.'

'Why not try sticking to your husband?'

Estelle aimed so high, Donald being much taller than she was, that she overshot the mark and knocked his forage cap away into the darkness. Then, without another word, she ran back to the kitchen door and locked it behind her. For what seemed an eternity, Donald hunted amongst the weeds and rubbish of that ill-tended area for his forage cap. Once he had found it he let himself out through the back door, found his way round to the road, and began his walk back to the camp.

He was assailed by the fear that Estelle might tell Bert who he was, clear herself by ridiculing him. He could become the laughing-stock of his unit. Then he fell to asking himself why he had rounded on Estelle. He would be making love to her at this moment but for Bert's arrival, although he had already known she was married. The thought of the delights he had forfeited so impulsively filled him with anguish.

As he trudged on, a feeling of despair overwhelmed him. Why did he so often take a fatal step, and discover the right

107

course of action only when it was too late? If only he could turn the clock back, not just this evening, but on the evening of his return to the north coast and others far back in time before then. Before he had reached the camp he had begun to wish he were dead, that he could come back as somebody else, that somehow he could make a fresh start in life.

"Ere comes the dark 'orse,' one of his companions called pleasantly as he neared his platoon hut. Donald raised an arm in greeting and gave a wan smile.

7

Angus enlisted in the Black Watch, where he found himself in the company of two other recruits from the northern Highlands who had been drafted into his platoon. One of these was Ewen Morrison, whose father had been a fisherman in Kinlochbervie, though now he was serving in the merchant fleet. The other, Hector MacLeod, was the son of a crofter like Angus and came from Assynt. This pair had a habit of speaking to one another privately in Gaelic, as Angus used to hear his brother Neil doing with their father Magnus. His new companions soon discovered that he could understand what they were saying, and it was not long before he had acquired a fluency in his native speech such as he had never enjoyed at home. In the alien world he had entered for the first time, this attribute of his identity became precious in a way Miss Cameron would not have guessed when she punished children for speaking Gaelic in the playground. It became a magic carpet on which Angus and his friends could sail away to their homeland, as they exchanged news and stories with one another in perfect privacy.

In the same platoon was an Englishman called Wright. How he came to be in a Highland regiment nobody enquired. By this spring of 1941 the territorial basis of recruitment in British regiments, long eroded, had been abandoned almost entirely. Wright was a thoughtful, observant little man who appeared not cut out to be a soldier, and all the more anxious to prove himself an efficient one. He treated the predominantly Lowland Scottish company in which he found himself with a kind of cautious deference. But the Gaelic-speaking trio aroused his active curiosity.

He would hover within earshot when they were passing the time in idle moments, and when they walked out of camp he would sometimes succeed in attaching himself to them without making himself in the least intrusive. If they entered a bar, Wright would always insist on paying for the first round of drinks, though he was not a great drinker himself. Neither Angus nor Morrison nor MacLeod ever passed an adverse comment on him in Gaelic, such as they often did at the expense of the Lowlanders. They tolerated him with sufficient respect, even though they were not always prepared to talk in English just because he was with them. There were, after all, generally far more youths around using his own language. If they refused to translate something they had said when he asked them, it was only because this would have been pointless. Jokes do not always translate well into another language. But although Angus and his friends never entered into a deliberate conspiracy to enjoy a joke at Wright's expense, the situation contained its own pitfalls.

One day Morrison took a photograph out of his paybook and showed it to Angus. It was a real photograph of a young actress, such as these lonely young men could easily buy in the shops. Angus took it and studied it appreciatively.

'Thanks,' he said to Morrison finally, and instead of giving it back to him he went off to rummage in his kit until he found a pin, then stuck the photograph up behind his bed. Morrison only laughed and went off to his own bunk.

'Who's the girl?' asked Wright when he was next in the vicinity.

'Oh that's the wife,' Angus told him in an off-hand way. Then, nodding towards Morrison who was sitting on the next bed, he added, 'Ewen gave her away.'

'Gave her away?' Wright echoed incredulously.

'Highland custom,' explained Angus shortly.

'You mean a sort of best man?'

'Sort of,' agreed Morrison, and there the matter might have rested, but for Wright's fatal curiosity.

He happened to enter their long dormitory as the three friends sat on adjacent beds, reading their letters from home. They liked to do this together because these letters were largely bulletins of local news, which they could share and discuss. Angus was propped on his own bed, reading a letter from his mother with the frown of concentration that was familiar to him on such occasions. Morrison and MacLeod sat facing him

110

on the adjoining bed, though it did not belong to either of them.

'You're looking worried,' Wright said solicitously to Angus as he passed, and hovered there for a moment. 'I hope that's not bad news.' Before Angus could reply, Morrison looked up from his own letter and intervened.

'Angie's wife is asking him to send more money home.' The three Highlanders knew perfectly well that they were all unmarried. 'It is not the first time,' added Morrison gloomily.

'Don't be foolish,' Angus said to him in Gaelic, and there, once again, the matter might have rested.

But Wright possessed a kindly nature, and his concern over the domestic difficulties of Angus were rekindled as often as he glanced at the photograph of the beautiful girl pinned to the wall above his bed. An opportunity to explore them occurred when Wright encountered MacLeod and Morrison on their own. They were walking rather fast along the parade ground, and his anxiety must have appeared all the more comic to them because he was almost at a trot as he fussed on beside them with his questions.

'Aye, it's bad, bad,' Morrison declared with a shake of the head. 'She will be selling the sheep. He had a boat too. She has sold that already.'

'Going with other men while Angus is away,' added Mac-Leod.

'You saw what she is like in the picture,' Morrison went on. 'I am sorry now that I gave her to him.' MacLeod could not help laughing, so that Wright turned to him incredulously. But it would not have occurred to MacLeod to explain that Gaelic nouns have genders, and a photograph is masculine.

'Why don't you warn him?' Wright asked breathlessly.

'We could never do thon,' Morrison replied.

'You could never say anything to him against his wife,' MacLeod confirmed.

'He would kill you,' added Morrison.

Wright allowed the pair to outpace him while he went off in another direction to think the matter over. He had heard Lowlanders in his Company declare that Highlanders were two-faced and treacherous. Morrison and MacLeod had spoken in a manner that sounded to Wright at least disloyal, even if it fell short of perfidy. They had suggested that Angus

Mackay might become violent, whereas to Wright he had always appeared the mildest of people. He certainly looked extremely strong, but his behaviour was as quiet as his speech. Wright's physique was almost puny, but he had been endowed with the gift of courage as well as sympathy, and it was his undoing.

He was obliged to wait many days before he encountered Angus on his own, not in the company of his false friends. But an opportunity presented itself when Angus lay on his bed, sewing at a button, while his two friends were chatting at the far end of the dormitory.

'Is your wife still asking you for more money?' Wright asked him, seating himself on the next bed. Angus merely sighed, and frowned with concentration as he pushed home the needle.

'Do you know why she needs more money?' Wright persisted, a look of desperate determination on his face.

'We have been losing sheep,' Angus told him in a dismissive way. 'There have been accidents.' He pulled the thread to its full length as he waited for a response, then inserted the needle again. What he said next revealed the thoughts that had flowed into the continuing silence.

'We have high cliffs at home,' he told Wright, 'and the sheep will be clambering down them to find the sweet grass on the ledges. Then they fall, and when we are out in the boat we find their carcasses floating in the water. We keep some of our sheep on an island, and when we go for them we find some on the island and some in the sea between.' He stopped, and still Wright said nothing. Angus glanced nervously down the dormitory to where his companions were bantering, as though begging them to come to the rescue.

'You've been losing your sheep all right,' Wright blurted out at last. 'Your wife's been selling them.'

'Of course she has not.' Angus turned to him in wide-eyed astonishment.

'Yes she has, and she's sold your boat too.' Wright pointed a small, accusing finger down the dormitory. 'You think those two are your friends, but they know and they haven't told you. They even know your wife's going with other men.' Angus dropped his needle and the greatcoat on which he was sewing a button, and leapt off his bed. He caught Wright by the clothing under his chin and almost lifted him off the ground.

'You dare come telling me things like yon,' he said quietly, his teeth glinting close to Wright's face. Wright stared back with slightly protruding eyes, his mouth kept shut by the thick fist of Angus beneath his chin. MacLeod and Morrison noticed the scuffle and came running up the passage between the beds.

'What's the trouble now?'

'He said my wife is going with other men,' Angus told him with slow fury, not letting go. His friends burst out laughing, then stopped when they realized how serious he was.

'But Angus, you are not married,' MacLeod pleaded with him. 'Let him go for God's sake.' He was speaking in Gaelic now, and Angus replied in the same language.

'Never mind that. He thought I had a wife and he said she was a whore. He said I had a wife who would go with other men.' Wright's stare was expressionless by this time, either because he could understand nothing or because he could not breathe properly. Morrison, who had said nothing, put an arm round Angus's jaw and jerked him back. Even if he was no stronger, he was considerably larger, and Angus let go of Wright in losing his balance. Perhaps unintentionally, he swung an arm out which caught MacLeod on the side of his jaw. Wright fled.

A chorus of cheers broke out at the sight of the three Highlanders apparently fighting, and this prompted them to sit down abruptly on the beds and engage in earnest talk, still using Gaelic. Those who watched were perhaps surprised by their hilarity, though they may have noticed that Angus appeared a trifle uncomfortable.

After this incident the trio would invite Wright to join them when they left the camp, and treated him as one they had learned to trust. They told him something of their lives at home, and listened in wonder when he described his own upbringing in a city of over a million people. Such congestion was not easy for them to imagine. Wright knew better by now than to ask them what they had said when Angus had him by the throat, nor did they ever inform him. Even when Angus removed the portrait from behind his bed, Wright said nothing. By the time they departed for north Africa, the trio had become a quartet.

☆   ☆   ☆

Their battalion sailed in to Tobruk on 11 October, to relieve the Australians who had been in the beleaguered city from the beginning. What made this autumn most different in the experience of the Highlanders from any they had experienced in the past was the noise. There was the smashed quayside of great granite blocks, the sunken river gunboat and the wrecked Italian warship. There was the stupefying heat. But whatever might be in the foreground, silence was the background of their world, and here there was no longer any silence, but ceaseless din as the backcloth to the havoc of that harbour.

They disembarked in frantic haste while German planes circled and swooped overhead, scrambling from the broken quay to firm sand, and up over a shingle ridge to the roadway. From there trucks carried them to the transit camp. On their journey, they gazed silently at the buildings of Tobruk, so new yet so derelict. But the transit camp was set in a lovely plantation of almond, apricot and prickly pear, under elegant waving palms. Here Angus found himself drinking tea made with salt water for the first time.

There was the plantation: there was the deserted city. There was the flat rocky country broken by wadis, curving off to desert, bounded by the sea. There were the days when they sat in their dugouts cleaning their weapons, and the days of ammunition and ration fatigues, which took them back to the harbour. After a month Angus knew that truck ride over the track which wound between winding clefts of the wadis, as well as he knew the coast road at home.

But he could not become accustomed to the noise. Enemy planes raided by day and by night, and the artillery of both armies answered barrage with barrage. Angus polished his bren gun until there was none cleaner in the battalion while he discussed the rumours with Morrison and MacLeod. They saw little of Wright any more, because he had been attached to another company.

The most persistent rumour told of a British offensive from Egypt, and it was followed by speculation that the Tobruk garrison would make an assault to join the relieving forces. The wise nodded over the accuracy of their prophecies when a mock assault was staged for the forces of Tobruk on 10 November. The trio learned that they were to have twenty-five Valentine tanks for their support. They had seen no-other armoured vehicles since their arrival save their bren carriers. Going into the mock battle at 0745 hours beside the comforting bulk of a twenty-five ton tank, they learned something more. Their company was the spearhead of the attack, and their section was the first over the starting-line.

Another ten days passed, while they strengthened the road-blocks on the Derna Road and discussed rumours that the advance from Egypt had failed. The emergency, when it came, was sudden and unexpected. Angus and his companions had just returned from a full week on the Derna Road, and they were unpacking blankets and greatcoats in preparation for a luxurious sleep. Angus took a last, admiring look at his gun, and he was adjusting the sights when the signal came. 'Bags' was the code-word, and there came a runner panting towards their positions, waving two sandbags.

'This is it,' said Morrison.

'And the best of luck,' said MacLeod sardonically.

They began to pack again. By first light they had reached their new positions a mile and a half within no-man's-land, and could hear the rumble of tanks advancing in every direction to their support.

Their platoon moved forward, about twenty yards behind its two tanks. The artillery dropped a protective barrage in front of them, and the enemy responded with every thunderbolt it possessed. The din was now such that everything Angus saw near to him appeared to be altogether silent, the corporal who looked as though he was calling something as he fell, the bullets that kicked up sand around him.

Then the tanks veered away to the right, and Angus saw that the moment had come at last for which he had left his home.

'If you want to fight, why don't you wear a uniform?' Donald's words rang in his head as he and his companions continued their steady advance. He noticed particular things in sequence, that it had become broad daylight, that he could see the enemy about 200 yards away, that the ground around them was not much damaged by artillery. Angus found that the effect of being under fire for the first time was to narrow his mind to a slit, unless it was the noise that did it. He looked around him, and it occurred to him that not half of his company were still on their feet.

'Down,' came the order, and although he had not heard it, he dropped with the others. It became apparent to him that they were caught in a mesh of fixed lines of fire. Morrison and MacLeod were still there with him, but there was no longer an officer to be seen. Then Angus recognized the Company Commander, lying not far behind him with what appeared to be a hail of machine gun bullets in his arm.

By now the tanks appeared to be miles away. There was no sight of the Piper, but would his music have been audible anyway? Angus began to feel lonely as they still advanced, crawling on hands and knees. Twenty-five yards from the German position they rose and ran straight for the barbed wire. They were caught in it by the time the Germans emerged with grenades, revolvers and machine-guns. Angus saw the platoon sergeant and two corporals killed almost on top of the enemy trench. His own uniform was caught in the wire but he tore it free, fell back a short way and flattened himself on the ground. It contained not a fold nor a tuft to shelter him. He found Morrison lying on his left side, MacLeod on his right.

Morrison filled the magazines of the bren gun as fast as he could, and as soon as it was reloaded Angus raised himself and released all thirty rounds in a single burst. As he did this, MacLeod ran forward to the wire, threw a grenade into the enemy trench, and immediately flung himself to the ground. There were cries from the dugout as it exploded, then another burst from the bren gun, and MacLeod rose again to fling another grenade. But the third time he did this, he was hit by a machine-gun over to the left and fell sagging into the barbed wire.

'Don't go,' shouted Angus at the top of his voice, although Morrison was still hardly a foot from him. 'There's nothing you could do, and you would never reach him.' The two youths just looked at one another, their faces taut, their eyes screwed up. Then Morrison handed Angus another magazine.

Angus tried to fire the gun but nothing happened. He adjusted it for gas and pressed the trigger again. Out came two rounds, then the mechanism stopped with a jerk. He had not raised himself to fire in a well-balanced position, and as his gun jumped backwards it knocked him flat again, where he lay tinkering, trying to discover what was wrong. Then he noticed his companion. Morrison was still lying in the same position, and he looked as though he were trying to pull a magazine from his pouch. But he had been sprayed from head to foot by machine-gun bullets and he was dead.

Angus could not touch him, could hardly look at him. Alone beside the enemy trench with his two dead companions, he forced himself to concentrate on the fault in his gun to the exclusion of anything else. It proved to be a stoppage in a million, caused by a broken piston rod. He had given the gun too much gas, and the pressure of the gasses coming back down the barrel had forced the piston group to the rear with the jolt that had thrown him off balance and saved his life.

At last Angus laid down his bren gun and turned to attend to Morrison. He laid him flat on his back as though he might be more comfortable in this position, and crossed his hands on one another. He took the papers and paybook from his jacket pockets and transferred them to his own. There was a strange silence, for no one had been left alive in the enemy trench and the machine-gun over to the left had ceased firing. Angus rose and walked slowly to where MacLeod was slumped in the barbed wire. He was very heavy to lift out of it and Angus nearly fell from weariness as he heaved the body free. He placed it on the ground in the same attitude as Morrison's, and took the papers from it also. Then he stood looking about him, weaponless. There was no one left to kill, only corpses in all directions.

No, not all directions. Wright's company was advancing, and when Angus ran over towards it he saw several of his own company who had joined it already. A lance-corporal gave him three grenades, and soon afterwards he picked up a rifle with its bayonet fixed. He found it increasingly difficult to measure time or distance.

There was the bayonet charge, the enemy rushing out of their positions and back in again, the cries for quarter ignored until not one of them was left alive. There were the streams of prisoners pouring past on their way to Tobruk. There were the rifles sticking up in the ground by their bayonets to mark where dead and wounded lay, the stretcher parties picking their way among them like lost souls in a blasted world. These sights alternated and repeated themselves until, late in the afternoon, Angus reached the point at which his battalion was to meet the British army coming to relieve Tobruk.

117

They were eight miles from the city by now, but no army came. There was no artillery, no ambulance convoy appeared, no ration truck. The survivors of that day were surrounded by the enemy on three sides. With nothing to eat, they prepared to survive a night under shellfire.

Angus was too exhausted to look for Wright, yet he did not rest. A biting wind from the coast cut through his khaki drill uniform as he dug with pit and shovel through the small hours, kept in motion by the temperature. It had become relatively silent. There were only the occasional burst of shells, punctuating the steady cry of the wounded out in the darkness. Many of them would be dying mercifully of the cold. Angus felt glad that Morrison and MacLeod were sleeping comfortably, suffering no pain, untouched by the bitter wind, unresentful that they were left unattended. He wondered as he staggered over his pick which fate his own would be,and which he would prefer, sudden extinction, or that painful breathing-space before the end. It was a hard choice, but then nobody was given the choice.

In the first light of dawn they began to run out to the wounded men, carrying any sort of covering they could find. While they were doing this, the enemy guns turned on them again, and two armoured cars caught fire with a burst. The few tanks scattered to escape the range finders. Some men were hit while the remainder huddled helplessly, hoping for the best.

Then, a little after nine o'clock, the convoy arrived. Blankets and greatcoats were thrown out, and presently the ration truck found its company. There was enough food to satisfy the hungriest. The truck had brought rations for the full complement of 140 men, and of Angus's company thirteen remained to consume it. A bottle of rum appeared, which Angus's companions passed from hand to hand as they relaxed in their makeshift dugout. But he had never tasted rum and could not bring himself to put it to his lips.

Gradually activity increased along the eight-mile corridor from Tobruk. Truck after truck streamed past them, towards others who were now fighting and dying as they had done yesterday, out in that wilderness from which they expected the relieving army to appear. The long processions of prisoners streamed past them again, shuffling toward Tobruk. Then there was a roar overhead as Tomahawks and Hurricanes shot past. Time slipped away as in a dream until, at four o'clock, Angus was detailed to go out with a burial party.

Angus was delighted to escape from inactivity and the thoughts it gave rise to. He joined a truck into which they lifted the bodies for conveyance to the cemetery in Tobruk. Not a face did Angus recognize, until they came to bodies lying in a strangely shaped heap, across one another. They were all Germans.

It was impossible to make out how they could have ended their lives in this tangle, and the burial party discussed the problem as dispassionately as they might have speculated on an incident in a game of football. But while they were offering their different theories, Angus caught sight of Wright. He was lying face downwards, and he had been hit in the back by a grenade. One little hand still held his tommy-gun in a firm grip. Angus turned him over, and for the third time opened the pocket which held a paybook. There was some Egyptian money in it too, a few stamps and some snapshots. The other members of the party had stopped talking as they looked at Angus.

'You get back, Mackay,' the sergeant said, nodding his head towards the escarpment where their position was situated.

'No,' replied Angus to the sergeant. But he did not help them to lift Wright's body, or any other corpse that day. He trailed about after them, and tactfully they ignored him. When they returned, there was food waiting, but he could not eat.

It was not that he was thinking of any personal loss in the deaths of his friends, or of his own survival. All that came to his mind were still pictures, and those of Morrisons and MacLeod were not gruesome ones. They lay with heads propped on helmets, dusty boots and gaiters splayed at an angle, grimy hands crossed in an attitude of rest. There was no disfigurement, only the little red marks in khaki drill. But the picture of Wright was hideous, and what made it so horrifying was that Wright had been pitched into this carnage with scarcely any asset except his courage. Only when Angus reflected that he could not have lain awake through that night of bitter cold did he feel any relief.

The din continued. The intermittent processions of prisoners passed back to Tobruk. The dusty convoys drove up the eight mile corridor. And retreating enemy transport began to appear on the distant escarpment road, pursued by the RAF.

But enemy tanks began to assault the long corridor, attempting to break through it, which resulted in Angus being despatched on a minefield patrol. There was a gap in their wire in which they dug holes for a dozen anti-tank mines. It had grown dark before their task was complete.

As they were running forward, each with his mine, they heard the crescendo of a truck approaching at great speed, although they could not see it. As fast as they could, they placed their mines and darted back towards their slit trenches, and in his haste Angus tripped. He had barely completed his headlong dive after the others into the trench when the roar of the on-coming vehicle turned into a tremendous explosion, accompanied by blinding light. Although somewhat shaken, Angus soon collected himself, and presently he left the trench with his companions to inspect the burning wreckage of the vehicle and make sure that all of its crew were dead. But he found himself watching the other members of the patrol mouthing their words while he still heard the explosion. In a short while he was enjoying complete silence.

What struck him most forcibly was the extraordinary privacy. The other steel-helmeted figures chattered and jostled around him, and did not disturb him. Back from his patrol, he found that he could hear again the voices of MacLeod and Morrison discussing the news from home, Wright telling them about life in a city of over a million people, while he watched others laughing and joking on quite other subjects. He awoke to another day in that barren wilderness, and its noise no longer disturbed him. As he peered over towards the ugly escarpment where British planes were harassing an enemy convoy, he could see the moors where his sheepdog lay on a distant outcrop, waiting for the next whistle. He could almost count the sheep beyond the winding track to long-exhausted peat banks, nearly obliterated by the heather.

Then someone would nudge him and shout the latest order in his ear, and sometimes he could just hear it, at others he simply followed the actions of others. So it continued until after the victory of Sidi Rezegh had been consolidated and the British army arrived at last to relieve the gallant garrison of Tobruk. Angus returned with his battalion and remained at Tobruk over Christmas and the New Year. But when the battalion sailed for Syria, he did not accompany it. He was sent to Cairo for medical treatment, a graded man.

8

During the time when Angus was undergoing his training in the Black Watch, Donald was launched on a very different sort of military career, one based on a particular aptitude that he had shown already at Stellmore. There he had not distinguished himself as a linguist, nor developed any enthusiasm for history. He had made heavy weather of Shakespeare and Tennyson. But at about the time when he began to understand the importance of cricket, he had also begun to earn favourable reports from his maths master.

Scanning Donald's school reports, Captain Hunter had paid little attention to these entries. He was more concerned with the housemaster's remarks about Donald's developing character than with his son's progress in the impersonal subject of maths.

'Bound to come in useful when he goes into the firm,' Sir William Jones had observed once, when they were discussing Donald's future. But that was all. Donald's particular flair certainly played no part in his godfather's calculations as he dropped the right word in the right ears, in his attempt to help Donald to obtain a commission in the Intelligence Corps. Nor could Donald himself have suspected that it would serve to make an officer of him.

He had travelled by train from the camp to his interview, sullen and afraid. He was expecting to be asked why, as an old Stellmoravian, he had failed to obtain a commission already. He was taken by surprise when the recruiting officers reminded him of his interest in maths, and went on to enquire whether he did crossword puzzles. He admitted with embarrassment that he did, wondering whether this revealed some fatal aberration, unfitting him to become an officer. But the members of the recruiting board merely nodded, and their faces revealed nothing but pleasure and satisfaction. When Donald received his transfer soon afterwards and informed his parents, he was careful not to reveal what questions he had been asked.

He would not have wanted his father to suppose that commissions in the Intelligence Corps were earned by doing crossword puzzles, as he would be only too apt to do. Fortunately Donald was presented with a ready means of protecting himself against any possible criticism from that quarter, when he discovered that he had entered a world of top secrecy. It was impressed on him with the greatest solemnity that he must give nobody the least indication of the nature of his work, and as soon as Donald heard this he realized how effective the message would be when he passed it to his father. He proved to be right. Captain Hunter concluded, and informed others, that his son was engaged in work of the highest importance. People were left to conclude that he might well be preparing to drop behind enemy lines on sabotage missions, or join the garrison in Tobruk. Captain Hunter became excessively proud of his son after the period of disappointment.

This could not have occurred if he had known that Donald's secret work was in codes and cyphers, especially as a very high proportion of the most distinguished cryptographers in Donald's new unit remained civilians, and many of those who did wear uniform were doing work that bore little relation to their rank. Donald himself had supposed that his Corps, so recently created, would have some kind of corporate identity resembling that of the regiment he had left. Instead he found himself surrounded by officers and other ranks seconded from all kinds of other corps and regiments, and from the Royal Navy and the RAF in addition, not to mention the civilians. There was a great deal of information for him to withhold from his father apart from the fact that this heterogeneous collection of people of both sexes was working for a branch of Military Intelligence that must never be identified. Donald was relieved that this was so.

He also found his new life-style more congenial than the old. Instead of the communal life of barracks, he enjoyed the privacy of digs in a small county town. Here he was boarded with an elderly couple who treated him with respectful formality and never asked him a question. The slogan that 'Careless Talk Costs Lives' was widely displayed by this time, and evidently people had become aware that something particularly secret was going on in their neighbourhood. How far away they could only guess, as buses transported Donald and others daily out of the town in the morning and back at night. They were driven to a large converted country house, in whose grounds huts had been built among the trees.

Donald was taught the rudiments of encypherment by mechanical means, the process of encoding and decoding, using substitution tables, and the basic structure of a foreign language he had never encountered before. Now he understood why he had been asked whether he enjoyed solving crossword puzzles, and about his interest in maths. This part of his training he found easy. But the language was quite another matter, because it was Japanese. However, he was only expected to learn how coded messages were constructed in a telegraphese version of that language. Even so, he was not much good at it.

He found himself working beside another recruit, seconded from the King's Royal Rifle Corps, who proved a brilliant Japanese linguist by contrast while he had no head for figures. Before their acquaintance could ripen he disappeared suddenly, and Donald was told that he had been transferred to another department of Military Intelligence. For the rest, he never discovered what the majority of people were doing in that hive of secret activity.

In due course a travel warrant was issued to him which took him to spend a weekend at another converted country house. He found an extraordinary variety of men billeted there, of all ages and nationalities, required like himself to pass a series of tests that would qualify them for a direct commission. There was an intelligence test, an interview with a psychiatrist, a fitness test in the gymnasium. Here a candidate in late middle-age found it impossible to climb a rope, and Donald wondered whether he would fail to obtain his commission on that account. Everyone was asked to speak to the assembled company in the hall for five minutes, given his subject as he arrived at the platform beside the presiding officer and his attendant judges. There was a candidate of uncertain nationality who arrived at the platform to be told,

'Your subject is cleanliness.'

'You must cleen your teeeth,' he stressed earnestly, and

paused. Then, after deep thought, he continued, 'It is so important as, as, as cleeening your booots.' Again he searched his mind, but this time in vain. With a glance of desperation at the panel of officers he returned to his seat. Whether or not he and the candidate who could not climb a rope were passed as officer material, Donald received his commission as a Lieutenant in the Intelligence Corps during the autumn in which Angus sailed to North Africa.

When Captain Hunter received the news, he wrote Donald the first letter in which he had ever betrayed emotion to his son. Lady Jones succeeded in persuading the Hunters to visit London for a dinner of celebration as soon as Donald was free to join them. It was the first time his parents had made the train journey south since the outbreak of war.

Never had Donald received such a boost to his self-confidence as this occasion provided. As he sat in their company wearing his new uniform with the two pips on either shoulder, he could feel the waves of admiration and approval lapping round him. It was enough for him to sit in silence, listening modestly as the Joneses either interrupted one another or both spoke at once. They knew how secret his work was, so that he hardly dared open his mouth. They could not have divined that the words of Estelle were ringing through his head.

'Of course you'll be an officer soon, won't you, Don?' He was startled when Sir William Jones interrupted his train of thought by echoing her prophecy.

'I knew you had it in you, Donald.'

His father, grown pathetically shrunken, treated him as an adult at last, an equal. As for his mother, he could see as she gazed at him that she was pleased for his sake and a surge of affection for her filled his heart. But there was a suppressed anxiety in her expression as well, so that he longed to tell her he was a non-combatant. The thought of his father's reaction helped to restrain him. He was obliged to catch an early train out of London, before the air-raid siren had sounded.

'He's so discreet,' exclaimed Lady Jones after he was gone. 'I'd just love to know what he does, but he doesn't give a thing away. And I'm sure it must be terribly important.'

In fact, Donald's contribution to the war effort was negligible, neither had he the least idea whether what anyone else was doing in that country house surrounded by huts had any greater value. It was their most closely guarded secret that they were reading Germany's top-grade enciphered messages. The means of doing this had been imparted to them by Polish patriots, of whom five had been captured in France and tortured to death in an attempt to find out whether the formula had passed to the allies. Each of them had died in agony without knowing whether one of his compatriots had cracked under the strain, rendering his courage useless. But the deciphered messages revealed that none had succumbed, and the authorities were making certain that if such as Donald should fall into enemy hands, they would not be in a position to divulge the vital secret. Even when intercepted messages gave notice of the bombing of Coventry, the city and its inhabitants were left to suffer without warning, lest the enemy should suspect that their most secret method of communication was being tapped, Not even Sir William Jones had the slightest inkling of this crucial, precarious asset.

'Everyone must contribute to the cause in whatever way he can,' he responded to his wife's remark. 'What was so upsetting for Donald is that he wasn't given the chance earlier. He saw everyone else doing their bit, while he was left doing nothing.'

'That's what I mean,' inserted Lady Jones in her fey voice.

'We can't thank you enough, Bill,' said Captain Hunter.

The two couples talked on, refuelling the brazier as though Donald was still with them, warming his hands beside it. Meanwhile he sat in his carriage as it carried him back to his digs in the blacked-out county town, more nearly the personification of their hopes than he had ever been before. He realized this and it comforted him, as he sat there reflecting on the day's events. But deep down inside him he knew there was an identity that did not correspond with their expectations or the precepts of Stellmore or the uniform he was wearing. What it was remained something of a mystery to him.

He returned to the routine hours in his hut in the woods, to the long rows of mathematical figures, the periodical struggles with the Japanese language. Only one distraction interrupted his concentration from time to time, causing him to stare along his red pencil. He had never been able to forget Christine's last words to him at the dance, and since he wrote to apologize to her they had been corresponding. They did not exchange letters often, so there was no reason why they should discontinue.

After his first note of apology, Donald's letters had been impersonal enough. They merely commented on Christine's news, item by item, in a manner that demanded more. So, when there was more to be told, she would send him a fresh bulletin.

Her parents, he learnt, had grown so fearful of her living away at the hospital, surrounded by the snares of a town, that they had persuaded her to return home. Young as she was, she was carrying out the duties of district nurse. They had been very late getting the peats in this year, partly because of the absence of young people, but also owing to the weather. However, they were home at last. Angus had gone abroad with his regiment, just missing Neil when he came home on leave. Neil's boat had been torpedoed, but he was among the survivors. So Donald could still picture the surroundings of his youth and those who inhabited it, while he sat studying cryptography, just as Angus did while he gazed across the rocky wilderness outside Tobruk. And the next chance to return to them fell to him.

His training over, Donald was given a posting abroad, accompanied by embarkation leave. He informed Christine, telling her he would be visiting his parents near Inverness and adding that he was sorry she was no longer there. She replied more promptly than usual, suggesting he should come to the north coast. Jean would be especially pleased to have him, all on her own and with no news of Angus.

The snow arrived early that year. As Donald's train made its morning descent to Inverness, he saw the great barrier of hills white beyond the glassy blue waters of the Moray Firth. Even the Black Isle was white almost to its shore-line. But he discovered on his arrival that the train to the north was running as usual, and the country buses meeting it at stations along the way. The snowfall had been recent, not heavy.

'I think I'll go up and see Jean Magnus,' he told his parents soon after he had greeted them, tactlessly soon.

'But you wrote that Angus is abroad,' Mrs Hunter objected.

'That's why I thought I would visit his mother,' Donald replied. 'She's all alone now. I'm sure you can understand.' It was a completely dishonest argument, and Donald was uncomfortably aware of the fact. His motive in going north was not to comfort Angie's mother.

'How kind of you, Donald,' his mother said. 'That is very thoughtful of you. Of course you must go.' Donald's sense of guilt increased until his father broke in.

'If the roads get blocked by snow you'll be stuck. You know what can happen. Don't risk it.'

'It may be the last I see of snow for a long time,' Donald said with a laugh. 'I think I'll take a chance on it.' This was the first time he had seen his father since the reunion in London, and Donald realized that now he felt completely emancipated from his authority. 'I was making enquiries at the station and they told me there shouldn't be any difficulty.'

Captain Hunter's inertia was growing with ill health. He merely grunted. But his mother could not resist a final plea.

'You won't stay too long, will you?' she almost begged. 'You have such a short time with us.' She was sitting looking up at him as he stood, and when he turned in her direction she looked suddenly different. The skin underneath her eyes was like crumpled tissue-paper and he was afraid she was about to burst into tears. She had a fragile, frightened appearance.

'Oh, Mummy, I'm sorry,' he said, and left the room abruptly.

'Whatever's come over the lad?' asked his father into the vacuum. 'Oh well,' he continued when Mrs Hunter remained silent, 'he's bound to be in a bit of a state, going abroad like this. I suppose we must try to humour him.'

But Mrs Hunter had sunk dreamily into her own reflections, so that there was a long silence before finally she broke it.

'You remember what happened last time he went up there.'

'Well, what happened?'

'I don't know, but something that upset him dreadfully.'

'Nonsense,' snorted Captain Hunter. 'You're always imagining things, my dear.'

'I used to think I must be,' his wife replied abstractedly, 'you told me I was so often.' She rose and followed to where Donald was unpacking in his bedroom. Little enough time remained in which to seek a fuller understanding with her son before he went abroad.

☆   ☆   ☆

But Donald discovered, when he reached Angus's home, that

128

he enjoyed this understanding already. It is not unusual for the young to take strangers into their confidence rather than their own parents, and the circumstances of Donald's upbringing had combined with his own nature to make him secretive with his mother and father. Anyway, Jean was bound to have known what he could not be coaxed into disclosing to Mrs Hunter. Such incidents as his drunken brawl at the dance soon became common knowledge in such a small community. And Jean established an atmosphere of entire intimacy with Donald as soon as he arrived by making clear to him that she knew what had occurred during his previous visit.

'I am sorry Angie is not here to welcome you,' she said as he entered her house. 'I would not like you to think he holds anything against you.'

'I behaved very badly,' Donald replied. 'I still feel ashamed.' He gave Jean a rueful smile.

'I have seen my own sons drunk, especially when they had a worry on their minds,' Jean reflected, 'and we all have things to worry us these days. Now you're to sleep in the closet. You'll find it warmer there.' And she opened the door off the kitchen that led to the little room in which Magnus and she had lain in earlier times.

'But won't you be cold upstairs?'

'Oh dear no.' So Donald put his bag in the closet, took off his greatcoat, and sat himself in the armchair on the left of the blazing fire as Jean gestured to him to do. Jean went to the sofa under the window, where she sat, hands in lap as she asked Donald how his father and mother were keeping.

'You're growing taller every time I see you,' she remarked. It was as though she was deliberately dismissing the subject on which she had given him her reassurance. Donald looked round at the familiar objects, the wooden press painted brown, the armchair in which he sat with its worn rexine armrests, the patches of linoleum on the floor. He thought of the furniture in his own home, then of the sumptuous house of Sir William and Lady Jones. He would have better than this to offer Christine.

'I hear Neil was home,' he remarked.

Jean told him how Neil's ship was torpedoed and how he was saved. Then she reached up to the tall mantelshelf and took down an airgraph letter that had curled in the heat from the fire.

'I had this from Angie,' she said, poring again over the minute writing, reduced to a quarter of its original size in the photograph. Finally she handed it to Donald. 'You read it yourself.'

He had never seen a letter from Angus, and he was surprised how firm and clear the writing was in the diminutive airgraph. He read that Angus was perfectly well, except that he was rather deaf, and was not with his battalion any more while he attended a hospital.

'Poor old Angie,' Donald said. 'I'm sorry about that. But it sounds as though he should be all right again soon.'

'He's alive, and that's enough to be thankful for,' Jean said with a sigh. 'Here, I'm forgetting to give you anything to eat and you must be hungry. But it's all ready.' Her way of banishing worry had always been to busy herself, Donald remembered.

'I'm glad you're here, Donnie,' she said as she laid food on the table.

He had hardly finished eating when Christine came in.

'Hullo Jean,' she said, pulling off her woollen gloves and throwing them on the press. 'Hullo, Donnie, so you got back.' She shook him by the hand as he rose from his seat at the table, then went straight to the fire and held out her fingers to the heat.

'What like was the road from the station?' she asked over her shoulder.

'There was some snow higher up the strath, but nothing much,' Donald told her.

'Will you take a cup of tea, Christine?' Jean asked.

'No I couldn't, thanks. I'm just after having tea.' She flung herself down on the couch and smiled at Donald.

'My, you look smart in your new uniform,' she complimented him. Donald covered his pleasure and embarrassment by moving back to Magnus's chair and seating himself deliberately. He was trying to find the right words in which to express his feelings at the sight of Christine when she turned to Jean and asked, 'Have you had any more word from Angie?' She shook her head.

'How bad do you think it is?' Christine asked Donald.

'If it was gunfire that deafened him, he should be all right again soon,' Donald guessed, trying to reassure them. But how could he know? 'I haven't experienced much gunfire myself, so I can't really tell,' he added. His words made a pool of silence.

'Neil was torpedoed, and he came home all in one piece,' Donald said as cheerfully as he could, and Christine laughed.

'How long are you up for, Donnie?' she asked him as Jean went out to milk the cow in the byre.

'I'll have to go back the day after tomorrow. My mother and father didn't want me to come at all. They said I might be snowed up.'

'So you might,' Christine replied with a smile, 'and then wouldn't you be pleased. But it doesn't look very likely, the way it's beginning to thaw.'

Jean confirmed this when she returned, carrying a can of milk. She placed it on the dresser while she tied a scarf round her head.

'It's a mild night,' she remarked.

'Don't bother taking that down,' Christine said to her. 'I can easily call at Jack's with it on my way home.'

'Be quiet,' Jean replied, picking up the can of milk. 'It will do me good to take a walk after being in all day.' She set off down the hill to where Jack's family lived in their house on the lower croft.

'What did your parents say about your coming out to meet me?' Donald asked as soon as they were alone. 'Or didn't you tell them?' He leaned back in Magnus's chair as comfortably as he could considering that the springs were gone and his uniform felt tight. He saw himself suddenly, sitting on the hard little sofa in Estelle's house, except that now he was dressed as an officer just as she had predicted. The memory buttressed his self-confidence in a curious way.

'I'm afraid they look on me as rather a lost soul already,' Christine replied flippantly. But when she noticed the effect of her remark on Donald, she added more seriously, 'Yes, I told them I was coming to see you and they sounded very pleased.' She paused, her dark eyes gazing thoughtfully into the peat fire. 'They're a bit like that,' she reflected.

'What do you mean?'

'Oh well,' Christine went on, without taking her eyes from the burning peats, 'you'd expect them to approve of me associating with someone like you, wouldn't you? They once told me that if we're not quite the gentry, we're a step above the commonality.'

Donald laughed while Christine continued to stare into the fire. Then he remembered the fight at the dance. Her parents were bound to have heard about it, or were they? He asked her, but she only shook her head.

'That was a long time ago,' she said cryptically.

'Then what about you and Angus?' Donald pursued, but Christine chose to misunderstand his question.

'We have known each other all our lives,' she answered, as though her parents' attitude was beside the point. Donald felt a surge of jealousy.

'But Angus never – he didn't ask you to marry him?' The question was so abrupt and uttered in such a strange way that Christine turned and looked Donald straight in the eyes.

'No, he never said anything about that,' she told him. There was a strained silence, while Donald glanced around at the furniture of this home that belonged to Angus, and then at the girl whose parents approved of him because he was a step above the commonality like themselves. He took his next plunge.

'Do you want to live here all your life, Christine?' His eyes circled the room again, as though here meant this house, the home of Angus. 'Would you be just as happy if you left this place altogether?' Christine turned back to the fire while she considered the question.

'Sometimes I feel I would like to clear out for good, but that's only when things at home get too difficult. I want to be free to live my own life, and perhaps I'll never be able to here. Or not until I'm too old to care. But if I leave, I'm not sure how much of me I could take away. I belong here, and that's all there is to it.'

Now it was her turn to explore the room as Donald had done. He watched her eyes as they rested for fractions of a second on the brass rail where no socks were hanging, on the ledges beside the fire where no boots were drying, on the shelf where the letter from Angus was propped, curled by the heat. Her glance flickered in his direction and was held by his expression. What could she read in it? Desire for possession? Jealousy? A desperate feeling of insecurity?

'Wait till you've seen more of the world,' Donald said with all the assurance he could muster, leaning back casually in his chair. But the effect of his remark was to concentrate Christine's mind on this little world of her own, and to share it with him as though she understood that it was what he really wanted too. Changing the subject abruptly, she told him about old Dugald who lived by himself up the hill, where Jean visited him regularly to make sure he always had a fire and enough to eat.

Dugald was very bothered by the black-out regulations. Once the policeman had lent him his torch to see his way home on a dark night. Dugald was afraid to leave it burning in the kitchen when he went to bed, in case it put the house on fire, so he left it in a bucket of water outside the door.

'That put her out,' he told the policeman when he came to collect his torch the next day. But the light of the torch in its bucket had been seen dimly by certain neighbours, who told Dugald that he might be accused of signalling to the Germans. This filled him with such panic that he nailed newspapers and sacking over all his windows, so that he had to light a candle by day as well as night to see in his home. At least until Jean next visited his home and set his mind at rest.

Jean herself returned from Jack's house as Christine was telling this story, and once again invited her to take tea. But Christine rose, and said it was time for her to return home. Donald said he would walk back with her, reflecting that he had never set foot in Christine's home, although it was so close to his childhood home.

The moon was out, lighting the headland and the deep bay. Beyond, the snow-line showed faintly along the high ground to the south. They walked across the sands well apart from each other. For one thing, their figures would be plainly visible in the centre of that great amphitheatre, from many of the houses scattered about the surrounding hillsides. Suddenly Donald stopped at the place in the bare expanse of sand where he had a picture of himself, vomiting while he leaned on the shoulder of Angus. He was one of those who remembered clearly what occurred when he was drunk, while others recall nothing.

'What is it?' asked Christine, while he stood as it were outside himself, witnessing the incident. He looked around, taking his bearings, wondering whether the moon had been as bright on that night, so that others might have witnessed it too.

'You look as though you'd seen a ghost,' said Christine with a laugh, and Donald stopped himself from replying, 'You're the one who's looking at a ghost.'

'I was thinking how beautiful it is here,' he said instead, and indeed this thought had swept away the other. 'I'd almost forgotten. This is certainly something you couldn't take away with you.' They continued their walk across the sand.

Christine's father had called his house Bethel, and this was the name by which he was known in a community in which all the Mackays needed by-names to identify them. 'O God of Bethel, by whose hand thy people still are fed.' Whether it was God's hand or Bethel's that was supposed to be doing the feeding, Christine's father sometimes officiated at public worship as a Church Elder when the Minister was away. As they were approaching her home, Donald suddenly recalled one such occasion from long ago. Bethel had climbed into the pulpit, stared down at the congregation, and startled them considerably by his opening words.

'You are all like an old table I have just thrown out of my house, full of dry rot.' Donald burst out laughing as he thought of it.

'What's the joke?' asked Christine.

'I was remembering one of your father's sermons,' he answered, but refrained from going into particulars.

'Which one?' He did not answer. 'Was it the time he took two steps to his right in the pulpit and said, "I'm going to heaven" and then two steps to his left and said, "Now I'm going to hell"?'

'No, I wasn't there that time,' Donald said.

'The joke was that from where the congregation sat heaven was to the left and hell to the right.'

They were approaching the house of Bethel and Christine turned right to enter her home as usual by the back door. But evidently her father had seen them approaching, because he emerged from the porch at the front which they seldom used.

'Good evening, Donald. Welcome to our humble house.' Bethel still possessed the handsome appearance that Donald remembered from so long ago, though his black hair was now flecked with white. He was speaking as sonorously as Donald had heard him doing from the pulpit, but then, he had spoken with the Hunters outside the church after public worship as though he were still addressing God. Donald wondered whether he talked privately with his family in the same tones. More urgently, he was not sure how he ought to address Bethel. By-names were never used to anyone's face: generally people used personal names irrespective of age. Bethel saved him from his quandary.

'Mrs Mackay will be sorry that she was out when you called. An errand of mercy.' All the same, he gestured to Donald to walk in through the porch, as the two shook hands.

'How are you, Mr Mackay?' Donald said without moving forward. 'Please give Mrs Mackay my greetings and tell her how sorry I was not to see her. No, I won't come in just now, thank you. I ought to be getting back to Jean's.'

He glanced from Christine to Bethel, wondering whether he ought to have called Jean Mrs Mackay as well. But Bethel appeared to be beaming with satisfaction over the distinction Donald had drawn between the mothers of Christine and Angus.

'I quite understand, yes indeed,' he pronounced majestically. 'But I hope you will visit us another time.'

'I look forward to that very much,' Donald assured him as convincingly as he could, and turned back to Christine. 'Shall I see you tomorrow?'

'I have some visits to make in the morning, but I'll come over in the afternoon,' she replied. Another swift glance at Bethel's expression of approval, then Donald said good night to them both and left. He felt a strange elation as he returned across the bay, following their footsteps in the sand which the incoming tide had not yet obliterated. He thought of Christine in the stifling atmosphere of her home, of how she must long to escape and how well-placed he was to rescue her. Far more so than Angus, who didn't seem to have shown any inclination after all. Or had Christine failed to tell him the whole truth? There was still the next day, to find out.

She appeared early in the afternoon, having changed out of her nurse's uniform after finishing work. Donald had abandoned his uniform also. The weather was mild though blustery as the pair walked out to the headland, passing the football field. The goal posts, which no longer had cross-pieces, swayed at intervals and the ever-spreading reeds in the bog beyond were bowed low towards the east. Donald and Christine climbed to the highest point of the headland, over grass cropped by the sheep and outcrops of rock, and stood by the small summit cairn to gaze in all directions. Christine's long dark hair blew across her face as she turned to watch the waves surging into the bay, then swept her eyes over the pewter sea towards the island.

'Were you ever on it?' she half sang into the wind.

'No.'

'Neither was I.' Then they scampered down to the narrowing point between bay and rocky geò.

'I wonder how Neil's boat is doing,' said Christine as they passed the place where the path ran down to the port. They peered down the precipitous scree where the zigzag track still showed at the embankments. Under the wall at the bottom Neil's boat lay upside-down beside the ruinous tarry hulk beneath which his lobster creels were stored.

'Can you imagine anyone carrying two sacks of meal on his back up that path?' Donald asked.

'He was a grandfather of my mother's,' Christine answered, 'or perhaps a great-grandfather. His name was Alec Fraser.'

'Goodness!' Donald blurted out without thinking. 'I bet Bethel doesn't go around telling people that.' Then he added quickly, 'I'm sorry, Christine. I oughtn't to have said that.' But she only laughed.

They walked on until they reached a part of the slope marked by no special feature.

'Angie once called this Donnie's brae,' Donald remarked. Christine stopped beside him and glanced around, mystified.

'Why on earth did he call it that?' she asked finally. Donald did not reply, but walked cautiously down the steepening grass until he could peer over the rocks below. Yes, it was the right place. There was the bent stratum of rock like a huge imprisoned spring, except that it was not so huge as he remembered it.

'Oh I don't know,' he said. 'We used to come out and climb the rocks here.'

They reached the end of the headland, where the sea heaved in its narrow channel between the precipice under their feet and the rock-island beyond. Spindrift larger than sponges blew up the chasm and scattered fragments over them. On such a gusty day they dared not stand too near the edge so they lay down, flat on their stomachs to mesmerize themselves with the sight of that eternal conflict between rock and water in the deep channel below.

'What a place to come for a holiday,' Donald exclaimed. 'Even if you left here, this would always be waiting for you.' He flung an arm round her shoulder, then glanced at the houses on the opposite side of the bay from which they could be seen and withdrew it again. But they were so close to one another that Christine's hair fanned his cheek. Would he be able to persuade her to leave here? To rescue her from the house of Bethel by whose hand was one thing, to ask her to share his exile, quite another. 'I'm not sure how much of me I could take away,' she had said. The real question was, how much would be left if she went. Come to that, how much of him was left? He became aware that Christine had not commented on his last remark. She was gazing abstractedly into the chasm as though she had no companion beside her. Boisterously Donald claimed her attention.

'Next time, you'll have to pay a visit to the south. We'll go to London and – oh – all sorts of places.'

'I'd like to do that,' said Christine, looking up with a smile at his sudden impetuosity. But when? He was going abroad, and Angus might return before him. He needed time, and there was so little of it, so little privacy either.

They rose stiffly from their hard couch above the chasm and wandered back along the headland. Now, when they could talk privately, perhaps for the last time, they said little, each apparently withdrawing from the other as if in preparation for the parting. But perhaps their thoughts were identical, both trying to reach a decision before they disclosed it to the other. At the path to the short cut over the sands Christine turned to leave Donald, at which he looked so crestfallen that she swung round and seized his hands in hers.

'I'll be back,' she assured him. 'I'll come over to Jean's after tea.'

'Shall I come and fetch you?' Donald asked, a note of desperation in his voice.

'I might never get out of the house if you do that,' she said. 'Don't worry. I'll come, I promise.' And with a wave over her shoulder she sped down the machair to the shore.

Donald returned to Jean's house with one decision taken. He would try to find out from her what she knew about the relations between Christine and Angus.

'Do you think there was anything serious between them?' he asked as casually as possible, when the opportunity came.

'Serious?' she echoed. 'They're only children, the two of them.' Donald thought, I suppose she thinks I'm still a child too, and while he paused she changed the subject.

'I'm sorry you only come for such short visits,' she said. 'Plenty people would like to see you. You grew up amongst us and nobody here forgets old friends.' Jean's words didn't sound as though they were meant as a reproof, more like reassurance. But they reminded Donald that he had scarcely thought of visiting houses in which he had been made welcome as a child, and he felt ashamed as well as comforted.

'Once the war's over and everyone's home again, I'll be able to come back for longer.' The word 'everyone' peopled the kitchen in which they sat. Then Jack's wife walked in, while Donald was eating his tea, and stayed talking for a while before she returned home with her can of milk. Christine arrived later than Donald expected, when he was beginning to fear she would not come at all, and soon afterwards Jean rose and announced that she was going to her bed.

'I'll have to be up in the morning or Donald will miss his bus,' she said with a laugh, though everyone knew she always rose early, whatever time she went to bed. The next moment she had closed the kitchen door and they could hear her steps on the stairs.

It came as a complete surprise to Donald to be left alone with Christine like this, and he began speaking erratically. In his confusion he talked about the firm of Hunter and Jones that would be his, the splendid home of his godfather in London that he would take her to. He spoke as though he was a knight in shining armour, come to carry her off to distant lands and pour infinite riches into her lap. Suddenly she had had enough.

'Oh do stop talking like that. Do you think I'm after you for your money?' It was like a slap in the face. Donald's eyes dropped to the linoleum floor while the silence lengthened between them. finally it was Christine who jumped up from the couch and sat herself on the arm of his chair.

'I'm sorry, Donnie, I'm sorry,' she kept repeating, and as she did so she lent over to take his head in her arms, as though she was a nurse again, tending a patient. She had large, beautiful breasts, almost but not quite out of proportion to her height. Donald snuggled into them, while one of his arms slid round her back. I mustn't make another mistake, he thought to himself, as he cautiously moved his other hand under her right breast.

'I was only trying to tell you how much I love you,' he whispered. 'The trouble is, you don't get much practice at an English public school.' They were both convulsed with giggles, their bodies vibrating as though they had only one between them.

'Let's go to bed,' he said, his heart missing a beat over the risk he had taken. Without a word, Christine rose from the arm of his chair and he propelled her into the bedroom off the kitchen in which he was sleeping. He did not look to see what she would do as he began to undress. But he still wore his trousers when he turned to take her in his arms and kiss her. She had already unbuttoned her blouse.

At Stellmore Donald had been warned more than once that if he masturbated he would go to hell, that he would probably become impotent, and that he would be expelled if he were caught. This was one of the few respects in which his training there had failed, though only partially, in that he never lost his sense of guilt as often as he infringed the taboo. This did not diminish the number of his lapses, once as many as seven on a single Sunday afternoon under Glendower's oak. He had returned to evening chapel at which the headmaster had referred obliquely and threateningly to the subject and it had seemed to Donald that his pince-nez was pointed directly at him as he did so. Since Donald never saw any evidence that any of the other boys shared his depravity, he could easily conclude that he was the only culprit. But the consequence was that this part of his physical structure functioned normally, like those which had been developed by batting a cricket ball. All that was wanting was the same team spirit, and Donald never suspected how many of the other boys had added this dimension to the forbidden sport.

'I've never done this before,' he confessed to Christine as they detached themselves and he began to unbutton his trousers. Not with anybody, he might have added. Estelle came to mind.

'Neither have I,' Christine assured him, continuing to

undress also. Each could well believe the other although she was nineteen and he twenty, and there are not many of this age who would care to make such a boast, or expect to be believed.

Donald had feared as he entered the bedroom that his apparatus might fail him and give Christine the impression that he did not really love her, truly desire her. When the time came to remove his last article of clothing, his pants, he was alarmed instead in case it gave her the impression that his love for her was mere lust. So he turned his back ungallantly, then leapt into bed before she could see him stark naked, and drew her in after him as soon as he could.

Jean had left a little lamp burning beside the bed. Donald raised himself to blow it out, and in so doing removed the last barrier of inhibition that divided them. So they found at last the cause that united them, the force beyond love that drove them on, the desperate need to slay the dragons of guilt that had encompassed their most natural urges ever since their adolescence. The triumph of their conquest heightened the ecstasy of their first fulfilment, and it was not much lessened by their fumbling ineptitude.

'We'll marry,' Donald whispered as they lay panting in one another's arms. 'I'll send you a ring from London as soon as I get there.' He felt for the third finger of Christine's left hand and fingered it as though measuring it for size. Then they began to make love again.

Nobody had told Donald that girls have orgasms like men, and he had already enjoyed two before he discovered it. The first followed his exploration of Christine's breasts, almost as soon as he had succeeded in penetrating her, the second his discovery that she did not mind him licking her nipples with his tongue. He was still relaxing when she moaned and become convulsed, spurring him to fresh activity. But this had only occurred once again by the time he was approaching his score under Glendower's oak. After that he must have fallen asleep because he was startled to feel Christine shaking him.

'Whatever's the time? Where are the matches? Quick, light the lamp.' Donald leapt out of bed and half opened the door into the kitchen, so that his naked body turned to gold in the shaft of light from its paraffin lamp. The room was still empty, the black-out curtain well secured. He darted in, picked up the lamp and returned with it to the little closet. He found that he did not feel shy, standing unclothed in its light before Christine's eyes.

'You get back into bed,' she said, springing to her feet. She pressed her body against his to kiss him once more while he still held the lamp, then began hurriedly to put on her clothes.

'I'll take the lamp back to the kitchen and then let myself out,' she told Donald as soon as she was dressed. 'Can you see anything wrong, anything they would notice when I get back home?' She turned slowly in a circle while he inspected her from his pillow.

'Yes,' he said. 'You're twice as beautiful and you're mine.' She gave a little wave, the door closed behind her, then the chink of light vanished from under the door as she blew out the lamp. Mine, mine, he repeated to himself in the darkness until he fell asleep.

Hardly a moment seemed to have passed before there were sounds in the kitchen again, the chink of light under the door, and then Jean beside his bed with another lamp and a cup of tea.

'There's no hurry,' she said. 'I hope you slept well.' His sense of well-being lasted until he got out of bed and noticed the blood on the sheets. He examined the marks carefully. Only blood. He dressed breathlessly and then waited until he heard Jean leave the house by the back door. She would have gone to the byre. He hurried through the kitchen into the scullery, seized the short potato knife and clumsily cut his finger with it. There was more bleeding than he expected, but he managed to contain it in his other hand until he reached his bedroom again. There he allowed some to fall on the sheet, and wiped the rest on the shirt he had worn the previous day, still lying over a chair. To his relief the bleeding stopped. He wound a handkerchief round his finger while he listened to the sounds that Jean was making, back in the kitchen. Then he came out with his safety razor, to shave in the scullery.

'I'm afraid I cut my finger,' he said to Jean, 'and there's blood on the sheets.' She looked him straight between the eyes until he dropped his own.

'I hope it will be all right,' she said, without asking to inspect his finger. He looked at her again and she was smiling.

'Sit in to your breakfast,' she said, 'or the eggs will be too hard. You can shave after.'

141

When Donald reached home that afternoon he surprised his mother very much by the affection of his embrace, and he was so high spirited in his father's company that Captain Hunter said to his wife: 'There, what did I tell you? You were imagining things, my dear.'

But although Mrs Hunter was relieved to see her son looking so happy, she pondered deeply over the cause. For his part, Donald agonized over whether to disclose it, but left without having done so.

9

He returned to London on the overnight train which deposited him in the morning, leaving him until four o'clock in the afternoon before he was due to catch another train to the west country. Or so he assumed, since the station was Paddington. He did know that he would be travelling east by plane during the night. His trunk had been sent on ahead by sea, and he was carrying all his papers and the small suitcase he was permitted to take with him. It remained for him to report to an office in Whitehall and to pay his farewell visit to the Joneses. As he strode out of the station into the Euston Road, bits of paper blew between his feet along the dirty pavement, but he was blind to the shabby appearance of brave, battle-scarred London. He was thinking only of the ring he must send to Christine.

At a jeweller's in Regent Street he lingered over a tray of them. As he fingered the different stones a succession of images floated through his mind, Christine standing by the cairn on the headland, her hair blowing in the wind, lying beside him above the chasm, warming her fingers at the peat fire, and the last picture of all, her face in a halo of light as she left the closet bedroom with the lamp in her hand. Finally he chose a ruby between two diamonds, gave the jeweller a note to enclose with the ring and the address to which it was to be sent, and paid for it by cheque. He had toyed with other rings, but this one cost as much as he could afford.

As he walked down Regent Street to Whitehall he was assailed by misgivings. Christine had never said that she would marry him, he recalled. But surely she must intend to, after what had passed between them. Would she wear the ring and tell her parents? Donald's heart sank as he reflected that their engagement would then become public knowledge and might easily reach the ears of his parents. They would be dreadfully hurt that he had not informed them, whether they approved or not. He debated whether to write to them, or confide in Lady Jones first to discover her reaction. Then he thought of Jean and agonized over whether she had guessed what had happened in her house. It was almost a relief to arrive at the pile of windowless cubes in reinforced concrete near the Cenotaph where he was due to report. What had appeared so infinitely desirable at the time, so inevitable and so simple, was a dream that was turning into a nightmare.

Donald looked across the road at the Banqueting Hall in which King Charles had spent his last hours before he walked out to his execution on the scaffold. Nearly everyone in Whitehall was wearing uniform like himself, given new identities, their private lives tucked away. He scanned a notice, then turned into the well-guarded entrance to the house of cubes. He showed his papers, obtained a pass and left his case. It gave him an extraordinary feeling of comfort to divest himself of the entanglements of life and turn into an anonymous, junior officer in the Intelligence Corps. A man in civilian clothes with only one arm and a row of medal ribbons on his jacket conducted him deep underground in a lift, then along a featureless corridor.

'Should I salute?' Donald asked his escort.

'It's not usually done in the building, Sir.' How simple human relations were, regulated like this.

They entered the office of Major Banningham-Miller. The Major was sitting back, balanced on the hind legs of his wooden armchair, the brass buttons of his tunic undone.

'Lieutenant Hunter, Sir,' said the escort and disappeared. Donald came to the table and stood to attention.

'Good morning, Sir.'

'Why didn't you salute when you came into my office?' was all the Major replied, glaring at Donald through horn-rimmed glasses. He swung forwards on to the front legs of his chair, resting his elbows on the desk.

'I'm sorry, Sir,' he said, and saluted. He wondered whether to add that he had not omitted to do so without taking advice, but feared lest this might be construed as impertinence. He smiled slightly as he recalled the false sense of security that had invaded him as he entered the building. Pitfalls lay in wait everywhere. The Major's stare wiped the smile from Donald's

144

face. Then Banningham-Miller glanced down as he rummaged through a pile of papers with efficient fingers.

'Ah, Hunter,' he said at last in an entirely different tone of voice, then allowed himself another pause before altering it still more. 'Yes, yes. So you're off to India tonight.'

By now Major Banningham-Miller was smiling at Donald, but he did not smile back. This might be another trap. Donald continued to stand stiffly to attention, his face expressionless, wondering whether he had heard a question that required an answer, or a statement. The Major became positively ingratiating.

'You don't need to stand to attention,' he said, but Donald continued to do so.

'Well, I hope you have a safe journey.'

'Thank you, Sir.'

'Now I expect you want to get along and see Sir William and Lady Jones. Give them my kind regards.' The Major pressed a bell on his desk, then rose to his feet. He shook hands with Donald.

'Good luck, Hunter,' he said, as another escort arrived to conduct Donald back to ground level. He saluted the Major without saying anything and left his office. As he was going up in the lift he recalled Bethel's remark that Christine had quoted to him, and smiled to himself again. Even though he was only a Lieutenant, in the eyes of the Major he was a step above the commonality. Except that this had little do with what kind of person he was, any more than his uniform did. And what kind of person was the Major, really, when he could be two such different people in the space of five minutes?

Donald collected his case and continued down Whitehall to the Houses of Parliament where he would meet Sir William Jones. Cocooned in the costume of his commissioned rank, saluting one passer-by and acknowledging the salute of another, stepping to the safety of his godfather's world from that of his friend Major Banningham-Miller, he gave an appearance of self-assurance that he was far from feeling. As he glanced at others on his way, he wondered whether they too were hiding insoluble problems behind their masks, what kind of people all those uniforms concealed. It occurred to him to wonder for the first time whether other boys at Stellmore had masturbated secretly, whether they had felt the same guilt. Everyone wore masks that kept them strangers to each other, even to themselves. Did Christine really know him, when he hardly knew himself? Did he really understand Christine?

He was still trying to assemble everything he knew about her when he entered the Palace of Westminster. With an effort he put her out of his mind while he wrote his name on a form to announce his arrival. Soon Sir William Jones came bustling down the corridor to meet him. It was lined by seats of red leather and led to the chamber of the House of Lords, which had been taken over by the Commons since the destruction of their own chamber by fire bombs. Sir William wore the busy smile that he always adopted when he emerged into the central lobby in which his constituents waited.

'Well well, Donald, so you're ready to leave.' He shook Donald's hand vigorously, then looked at the gold watch in his waistcoat pocket. 'Just in time to go for lunch. You saw Banningham-Miller?'

'He asked me to give you his kind regards.'

'Capital fellow. You know it was he who got you into the Intelligence Corps. Of course he's waiting to get into Parliament himself. The next bye-election and he'll be in. Couldn't have found himself a better perch while he waits. That's why I knew he'd be able to work the oracle for you. Good at that sort of thing. There'll be no stopping him when he gets into politics. He'll probably end up on the woolsack. They say he isn't much of a lawyer but he's clever enough in other ways to do it.'

Sir William's voice boomed on among the gesturing figures of dead statesmen on their plinths either side of St Stephen's hall as they strode down it. Without Lady Jones to interrupt him, it seemed as though he could go on for ever. They walked across to the street behind Westminster Abbey which Donald had seen last when he met his parents in the home of the Joneses after obtaining his commission. There he sat down to his last meal in their company before his departure. He turned his head from side to side like a spectator at a game of tennis as they filled his ears from either side of the polished table. How could he tell them about Christine?

'I hope your mother and father were well when you left,' Lady Jones said.

'Father's not keeping too well, but I'm sure he'll pick up when the warm weather comes.'

146

'Of course they ought to live in the south, I've told them so again and again,' said Lady Jones. 'I don't know how anyone can live up there in winter.'

'They must have been sad over your going abroad,' interrupted Sir William.

'Yes,' Donald muttered, staring at his plate, and the Joneses exchanged one of their rare, silent glances, as though approving of his reticence. But he was thinking of how he had said goodbye to them without letting them know that he had asked Christine to marry him. Here was his opportunity to make amends by telling the Joneses. He could tell them he had been afraid of upsetting his father when he was unwell, ask them to break the news if and when they thought fit, test their reactions. He looked appealingly at Lady Jones and was about to speak.

'Never mind,' boomed Sir William jovially, as he watched Donald's expression of misery. 'You'll soon be back, and then we'll have you in the firm.'

'And you'll see all those wonderful places in India,' broke in Lady Jones, 'the Taj Mahal and – ' she tried to think of other sights without actually pausing – 'and the Himalayas and all those things. How I envy you going east.' She sighed like waving palm trees and minarets shimmering in pink sunsets.

'Yes, it will be fun to see the world,' Donald agreed. But he had lost the chance to tell them about his world, in which the pink sunset blazed from behind an island he had not yet visited and touched hilltops still covered with snow, even if they were not so high as the Himalayas.

'I've put a hundred pounds in Grindley's Bank for you,' said Sir William as he rose from the table, looked at his gold watch again, and assumed his characteristic air of bustle. Donald wondered whether he would have time to go to the bank, return to the jeweller's, and buy the more expensive ring that he had been unable to afford.

'Stay here till you catch your train unless you've anything else to do,' said Lady Jones as soon as Sir William had left to return to the House of Commons. 'I'll come and see you off at the station.' Donald turned to her gratefully and saw eyes filled with affection and pride. But what would they register if he told her about Christine? Once again he was given an opportunity to find out, and he let it pass. He said to himself by way of excuse that the person on whom Lady Jones lavished her love and admiration was somebody she had invented for herself, not him. He must not shatter the illusion, not yet.

So instead they talked inconsequentially until it was time to travel to Paddington by taxi, since petrol rationing prevented the Joneses from using their car for inessential purposes. For the most part Donald was only required to listen, his only difficulty to keep his mind from wandering as he did so.

There was a reserved carriage for Donald's party at the Paddington train, so that he was able to see at the outset that it included two Generals, a Colonel in Guards uniform and a civilian. Lady Jones knew who all of them were and whispered their names to Donald. After telling him that the Guards officer was a famous travel writer, she went to speak to the civilian, to whom she introduced Donald. He proved to be an expert on locusts, something to do with the Colonial Office.

'My word, you're travelling in distinguished company,' said Lady Jones when he left them. 'I didn't realize you were so important. Wait till I tell your parents. They will be so proud of you.'

'You mustn't tell them anything,' Donald replied, reflecting on what she might have told them if he had given her the chance.

'No, of course you're right,' she agreed. 'It's all terribly secret.' They stood on the platform in an embarrassed silence, as though to say anything might cost lives. Then Donald took Lady Jones in his arms in a surge of gratitude and affection. She was so pretentious and silly, yet so good and kind. He remembered that all his life she had loved and spoilt him.

'I'll never forget all you have done for me,' he said, kissing her on the cheek. 'Goodbye, Aunt Lucy, and thank you more than I can say.' She looked up at him with misty eyes.

'God bless you, Donald,' she said huskily. Then she turned abruptly and trotted away down the platform. Watching her departing figure, Donald thought how brittle she looked despite her mink coat. He was relieved that he had said nothing to alter her image of him. With only a few words he might have shattered her to fragments. He entered the carriage and seated himself diffidently in an empty seat after placing his case on the rack above. He knew that he was the one absolute nobody in that company.

The other occupants of his compartment not only ignored him: they showed no interest in one another either. By the time the train started on its journey the civil servant was studying sheets of typescript, the author dressed as a Colonel in the Guards read a large book, the Generals slept. It took them nearly two hours to reach their destination, when a truck carried them through total darkness to a jumble of huts. There they waited in a bleak room where Donald found himself shivering with cold.

'You'll be warm enough tomorrow,' one of the Generals barked at him cheerfully, and then the Civil Servant came and discussed the route they would be taking. Tea was brought to them, at which point the Guards Colonel made his appearance, dressed now in travelling clothes. The locust expert eyed him with hostility.

'Have you brought one of your own books to read on the journey?' he asked. The world-famous author did not reply.

It was almost midnight before they were told to embark, and Donald dragged his feet sleepily out of that bare waiting room. A chill wind blew out of the darkness, over the scarcely visible airstrip, so that he had to hold on to the peak of his cap with one hand while he pressed the collar of his greatcoat beneath his chin with the other. In front of the straggling party loomed the monstrous silhouette of their plane. Inside it the locust specialist came to sit companionably beside Donald, while the experienced traveller ignored the seats and made a nest for himself amongst the freight further forward.

There was a roar, a gathering momentum, and they had left British soil. Donald strained his eyes at the window but could see nothing in the blackness below him. Still he gazed, until at last the moon shone between clouds, showing him a peninsula of land and islands beyond it.

'Are those the Scilly Isles?' he asked, turning to his neighbour. But the locust specialist had already fallen asleep. Donald continued to look until the last scrap of land disappeared from view and there was only a silvery waste of sea, then he closed his eyes too.

He dreamt that he was reaching his destination. At first there was only the sea, lit by the moon. Then the island appeared beneath them and, as they began to lose height, the headland also. he had never landed in a plane before and gave a twitch of anxiety which half-awakened him. But he was determined to return to his dream,. He clung to it and it remained with him. The tide in the bay was far out as the plane landed on the sands without so much as a bump. Christine was waiting for him as he disembarked and he threw his arms round her and kissed her. She was wearing a mink coat.

'I'll never forget all you have done for me,' he said.

'Hullo, Angus,' she said, laughing with joy at the sight of him. Behind her stood Donald's mother smiling. He drew back from Christine to greet her.

'I'm not Angus, am I?' he said to her, laughing. 'Tell Christine I'm Donald.'

But his mother shook her head, and her expression became sad. The skin beneath her eyes was like crumpled tissue paper.

'Don't be foolish, Angie,' said Christine. 'Donnie went away.' Then suddenly she raised her voice to a shout. 'I'm forgetting you're deaf. Can you hear me now? Donnie went away.'

His mother burst into tears and began to run away along the sand. Donald struggled past Christine to reach her.

'Steady, old man.' It was the voice of the locust specialist in the seat beside him.

'I'm terribly sorry,' Donald mumbled. 'I think I must have been having a nightmare.'

'Don't worry. A lot of us do these days.' Donald could scarcely see the outline of the bald head so near his own. But the deep, calm voice was familiar and comforting. 'Just try to forget it.' Donald went to sleep again.

He was awakened by bright sunlight in time to see a very different kind of headland below him, arid rock that divided blue sea from an ocean of desert. Shortly afterwards they landed at an airfield near Oran.

Donald had never experienced such heat, nor such brightness. He stepped out of the plane blinking in the glare and almost stifled by the hot currents of air that welled up from the sandy ground. Looking about him, he saw huts scattered about the empty waste, but nobody to direct him. The other passengers were evidently accustomed to this route or others like it, and perhaps they supposed that Donald knew his way around as well. In his eyes they were far too senior in age and rank to consult. With what assurance he could muster he strode to the nearest of the huts, and discovered that it was a wash-house. He stripped to the waist, panting, to remove his vest and pullover, fearful lest this was the domain of other ranks, in which a Lieutenant ought not to be discovered naked by a Private. It did not look like officers' premises, and if it were, then why had the others not come here also? But nobody appeared.

Trying awkwardly to conceal his discarded clothing under one arm, he came out into the sunlight again. This time he saw a man in tropical dress near enough to call to him, 'Where are the others?' An arm waved towards a hut to his right. Here he found them all sitting down to an enormous breakfast of bacon and eggs, such as nobody saw any more in ration-controlled Britain. Only the locust specialist nodded to him as he put his winter clothes on a side table and took his seat.

Last night's dream returned to him and troubled him deeply. Had Christine accepted him only because Angus had been away and he was there, in Angie's home? Had she told him the truth about her feelings for Angie? Surely she would not have made love with him if it were Angus she loved. She was not another Estelle. But then Donald realized that she had never visited his own home since they were small children. She knew him only as someone in Angie's home, a member of his family circle. How would she have responded to him if they had always met in the home of the Joneses? He remembered the picture of her standing on the sands, wearing Lady Jones's mink coat, the way she had responded when he had tried to impress her by describing her affluent world.

'Oh do stop talking like that. Do you think I'm after you for your money?' What was she after that he could offer her? What would be the life that they could share together? Not that of the house of Bethel, not of the mansion of Sir William and Lady Jones. Each was an only child. Both had been imprisoned in the world of their parents. They had escaped into each other's arms, but where would they go?

When they had finished breakfast they were asked to return to the plane. There were more men about when they emerged from their hut, all wearing bush shirts of khaki drill with open necks, many of them in shorts. Their faces and knees were brown. The temperature in the plane was like a cool, soothing hand on Donald's brow.

They flew over desert, then over sea, then over desert again. Their journey lasted all day, and it was dark before they dived towards the lights of Cairo. A city blazing with light, and containing Angus. Here was the one person in the whole world in whom he could confide, attending the military hospital. Would Donald be able to meet him privately, although he was a Private? Angus was deaf, and Donald could hardly shout his secrets in a public ward. But perhaps Angus was so deaf that he would have to communicate with him in writing, even though he had not given that impression to his mother in the airgraph letter. Donald's heart sang, despite his misgivings, over the prospect of seeing Angus again. It seemed to him the most providential thing that had ever happened to him in his life, that he should be about to meet Angus, of all people, in Cairo of all places, just when he needed him so desperately.

The plane landed in the darkness, and its passengers were driven to a hotel on the outskirts of the city, where the Colonel-author was received more obsequiously than the Generals. Donald slept for the first time under a mosquito net, and when he woke he saw through his window the Great Pyramid on the brow of a sandy slope. The sun threw it into sharp relief, pink against a pale blue sky. Donald unpacked his tropical uniform of khaki drill and put it on for the first time. He looked at himself doubtfully in the mirror, feeling bewildered. He had not expected to be so alone on this journey, so isolated from anyone who could advise him.

He went to the breakfast room, where he saw the two Generals sitting at the same table. Taking a deep breath, he walked up to them.

'Good morning, Sir,' he said to neither of them in particular. 'Would you please tell me whether I ought to be wearing my sam-brown?' They did not snub him. Indeed, one of them gave him an amused glance, his spoon deep in a slice of water-melon.

'It doesn't really matter. Where are you going this morning?'

'I have to report to GHQ.'

'Do you know where that is?'

'No, Sir.'

'Well I'm going there myself, so I'll take you.' Perhaps life was simpler, after all, than Donald made it.

He went to eat his breakfast at another table after thanking the General, and set off soon afterwards by car, the General chatting about Cairo and the war, then asking Donald about his life in the army. They were driving along a broad straight road.

'Funny to think,' remarked the General, 'that thousands of years ago the funeral of Rameses or somebody may have taken this very route out to the tombs.'

'He certainly left something to remember him by,' Donald ventured. He was wondering where the Sphinx was, and whether he would have time to see it. But more important by far, he must find the time to see Angus at the first opportunity.

At GHQ the two men parted. Donald learned that he would be travelling on early the following morning, then he asked the whereabouts of the military hospital and took a taxi to it. As he tried to arrange the approaching conversation in his mind, Donald was assailed again by doubts about the relationship between Christine and Angus. He wondered whether he should tell Angus only that he had asked her to marry him, or whether he ought to disclose that he had made love to Christine. It would not be fair to her, perhaps, but it would be the one certain way of making the situation clear to Angus. Or would it make such a crucial difference? If Angus were in love with Christine, what would his reaction be when he was told he was not the first? Donald tried to imagine his own feelings, if he had been in the position of Angus.

He reached the hospital, where he gave Angus's name, regiment and rank. He was asked for Angus's military number, but despite his flair for figures, he could not conjure up the row of them at the top of the airgraph letter. He waited and waited, his mind now a complete blank. Then expectancy leapt in his breast as the orderly to whom he had given his particulars returned.

'Private Mackay was drafted back to England two days ago,' he was told. 'Sir.'

'Two days ago,' Donald echoed as the orderly turned to go, then called after him. 'How was Angus when he left?' The orderly gave him a surprised look.

'Private Mackay, Sir? I don't remember but he had the bottom medical grade and we couldn't do anything for him here. It was his hearing.'

'Thank you,' said Donald, recovering himself. He walked out into the intense sunlight and took a taxi back to his hotel. He had not told his parents, then he had not told the Joneses and now he had not told Angus. Each time he had felt guilty because he had failed to do so, then relieved that he had said nothing that might have upset them. So it was again. Distraught though he was to have missed Angus by such a narrow margin, he could take comfort in the knowledge that he had been prevented by this accident from hurting him. He flung himself down on his bed, naked in the heat, lost in thought that took him nowhere. He pictured Angus, returning home on sick leave, but this thought led him nowhere either. Oh well, he concluded, perhaps by the time I come back all my problems will have been solved by others. And perhaps that is best.

He roused himself, and thought of the Sphinx. Had it not gazed at the riddle of life since the beginning of recorded history? What would he be able to read in its ravaged features? He dressed, enquired at the desk, and learned that the Sphinx was only a short walk away, up the slope behind the Great Pyramid. He shuffled there slowly, his spirits numb in the heavy heat. Egyptians in grubby, colourful costumes importuned him to take camel-rides, to buy souvenirs, employ them as guides. Shaking them off, he walked to where he could look the Sphinx directly in the face.

The shadows moved slowly across that ageless countenance. Donald could read nothing in its expression, but it seemed to him that he was being scanned himself, and as he continued to stand motionless, submitting to this scrutiny, he felt a strange sensation that he was being lifted from where he stood although his body remained there, and dissolved in the flowing waters of time. Another Egyptian guide approached him, and the spell was broken.

He was called at three o'clock the following morning, and his party had boarded their aircraft before dawn. Donald was particularly sorry that it no longer contained the locust expert, the last tenuous link with the world he had left. He had said goodbye to Donald in the hotel hall, after his return from the sphinx.

'I'm terribly sorry you're not coming with us,' Donald had said to him, whereupon the locust expert had studied him for a moment, thoughtfully.

154

'Life is full of such passing encounters,' he had said gently, 'particularly in wartime.' It was as though he was commenting on Donald's relations with Christine.

In his place a young woman bound for Chungking had joined the party. To Donald's surprise they did not return to the airfield to board their plane, but were driven to the water's edge where a launch waited to carry them to a seaplane. Dawn broke as they soared towards the Sinai peninsula and the Dead Sea.

Donald experienced a serenity such as he had not known since his early childhood. He had severed the last links with his former life and all its entangling problems and felt as though he was in limbo, before being processed into some new existence. He had first become aware of this, he reflected, as he stood before the Sphinx, and his parting with the locust expert had snapped the last thread that bound him to the past. The harm he might have done during the past he had been prevented from doing, partly by the accident of circumstances, partly by his own indecision. Now everyone he knew was beyond his power to help or to harm.

They landed on the Dead Sea, where the heat was more stifling even than it had been in the desert. There they sat above the leaden water while mechanics came and tinkered with the starboard engine of the seaplane. At last they took off again, and lumbered towards the high barren mountains, beyond which lay the Persian Gulf. Donald alone showed no awareness when the starboard engine spluttered and then cut out entirely. But none of the occupants of the seaplane had long to concern themselves about this before it dropped out of the sky among the sharp ridges of that barren land.

10

Angus squatted beside his motor-bike, propped against the end of the stedding beyond his home. He had arrived on leave the previous evening and spent much of this day trying to put the long disused bike back into working order. Petrol rationing would prevent him from making much use of it but it was precious, and needed to be looked after.

The sloping ground between his house and the stedding had turned to deeply rutted mud during the wet weather of the new year. Now it was frozen hard. While Angus bent over his bike, his sheepdog lay motionless at a little distance, watching his every move. The dog's coat was not long, and silky black except for the point of his tail and his paws, which were white. He had a nose as sharp as a fox, and that nose and the two eyes behind it had been trained on Angus ever since his return. Nobody had taken him out to the sheep in the moors since the previous November.

The hillsides were spattered with great patches of snow, turned crusty by sun and wind. They were not melting, but evaporating slowly. Angus had given the cows an outing, except for the one that was heavy in calf. She happened to be the leader, and the others soon rejoined her, tiptoeing guiltily behind the back of Angus. His dog raised his head expectantly, but Angus allowed the cows to heave their way back into the stedding without calling on his services. The dog dropped his head again and continued to wait patiently.

Angus looked tanned and fit, but there was a drumming in his ears and they often ached. Sometimes he became giddy. If somebody spoke loudly, close to his ear, he could generally hear, but the effort of listening tired him.

Looking up, he saw the mail bus approaching the village along the coast road from the east. It came in sight behind the bay, under the high rocks, and lost speed as it climbed the other side of the post office. Angus straightened himself and gazed thoughtfully at the bus as it reached its destination. He turned to consider the bike again, gave it a kick start or two until the engine roared, then switched it off and strolled over to the house.

'Are you there, Mam?' he called. Her head appeared at the back door. 'I'll take the bike over to the office for the mails.' He scrubbed his hands at the scullery sink before going upstairs to change his clothes.

'Be sure to wear the balaclava,' Jean advised him as soon as he returned, but he did not hear her.

'Where's my balaclava, Mam?' he called, searching in corners. She went through to the closet, took it out of a drawer and brought it to him.

'Are you sure you want to go?' she asked, putting her mouth closer to one of his ears. Jean was not a person who found it easy to raise her voice. 'There's frost in the air and Geordie the Post can bring the mails in the morning if there are any.'

Officially, the mails that arrived on the evening bus were supposed to be delivered the next day by Geordie on his bicycle. But as a rule somebody would go to the office from each of the cluster of houses in that scattered community, to collect the post after the mail-bus arrived. They would stand about, chatting, until it had been sorted. It was one of their social diversions, more ecumenical than the gatherings after Sabbath services when people were separated by their different denominations. Nobody approved of this arrangement more than Geordie the Post, who had actually been known to scold somebody to whom he had been compelled to deliver a letter on the following day. All that way on his bicycle, just to deliver one letter, he had complained.

'I'll be all right,' Angus reassured his mother. 'I'd like to say hullo to people now I'm back.' His dog, hovering beside his bike, saw him mount it and resume the old routine of collecting the mails. In his frustration he made to chase a cat out of the straw by the stedding door, but when the cat hissed and put out a claw he thought better of it. Instead he went to chase the hens, which fluttered in all directions, undignified in their indignation.

The post office stood between the inn and the village hall, on the crown of the road which descended eastwards to the bay and westwards to the river mouth. There were already about a dozen people in it when Angus leaned his bike against its wooden wall and entered, although the sorting had hardly begun. A few of them he had seen already, the rest he greeted with a handshake and a smile. His mother had been right. His ears were aching painfully, and although he pulled off his balaclava he could hear nothing but a roaring noise.

'I'm sorry, I'm deaf,' he said, and then they shouted louder until he winced, still unable to distinguish more than a few isolated words. Geordie the Post was standing behind the counter, tucking letters and papers into the different cubby-holes on the wall behind him. Evidently he had noticed Angus's predicament and deliberately picked out his mail from among the rest, because he stretched an arm past the crowd of people and placed in his hands a letter for Jack's wife, a bill and the local weekly newspaper.

'Was Christine in the night?' Angus asked Geordie, who shook his head.

'But she had the wee parcel,' somebody said so distinctly into his ear that he heard it. Another winked at Angus and everyone laughed. By this time he had acquired the habit of joining in merriment that he did not understand, so he grinned with them. Then he left the office, put on his balaclava, and remounted his bike. He seemed to hesitate as he swung it back into the road, then he turned it, not eastwards towards his home, but west towards the river mouth.

It was not a very dark night, and since Angus's headlamp had been reduced to a small slit in accordance with black-out regulations he could see the river winding for some distance up the strath. He passed Donald's old home, now lying empty, as its present owners came to it only in the summer. Beyond lay the path that led through sloping fields to the house of Bethel. Angus parked his bike at the gate, to walk the rest of the way, and it was Christine herself who came out to meet him, alerted by the sound of its engine.

'You're a stranger,' he said, putting an arm round her waist and spinning her back into the house. 'Where have you been hiding since I came back? You'll need to speak up when you think out an excuse, or I shan't hear.'

They were in the kitchen, where Angus flung himself down

on the settee and gazed around with a happy grin. Christine's home was the same kind of solid stone croft house as his own, but the old open fireplace in the kitchen had been replaced by a small one of glazed tiles, and above it hung the text: Straight is the Road and Narrow is the Path, and Few There Be That Enter In. The ornamental dresser opposite contained a mirror that doubled the light of the paraffin lamp.

'Are your mother and father in?' Angus asked, nodding towards the room at the other end of the house.

'No, they've gone visiting the Minister,' said Christine.

'That's fine,' said Angus, who had not heard her, but had seen her shaking her head. In his ebullient mood he was slow to detect that it wasn't fine at all. 'Don't stand around where I can't hear you,' he went on. 'Come and sit here beside me.' He took her hand and gave a pull so that she over-balanced and nearly fell on top of him.

'Now what was all that they were saying in the office about a wee parcel?' he asked her. He was taking up the threads of his relationship with Christine as though he had never been away, had seen her yesterday.

'Did they tell you about that?' replied Christine with a startled look. 'What did they say?' Angus had heard nothing, but he had noticed her expression. He gazed at her thoughtfully for a few moments, then broke again into his broad smile.

'You're as bad as the rest of them,' he chided. 'I couldn't make out what they were getting at, and now I cannot hear you either. You laugh at me behind my back, the lot of you, and tell me nothing at all.'

'There was nothing to tell you,' shouted Christine, putting her mouth close to Angus's ear. He turned quickly and kissed it, just brushing it with his lips.

'Oh yes there was,' he persisted mischievously. 'There was a wee parcel, and they thought I had sent it to you. Was it this size?' He held his two stubby index fingers six inches apart. 'Or was it smaller?' He brought them to within an inch of one another.

'I'm not telling you,' she said, turning away her head, so that Angus did not hear. Perhaps she was prolonging the suspense for fun.

'Well, if you don't want to tell me anything,' he said with mock solemnity, 'at least I can read the paper.' He drew the local weekly out of his pocket, broke the wrapper, and opened the double sheet, holding it towards Christine so that they could share it. When she did not respond he turned straight to the column that almost everyone read first, the one in which war casualties were reported. Suddenly he broke the silence.

'Donnie's been killed. It says here, "Donald, only son of Captain and Mrs Norman Hunter." That's Donnie and he's been killed.'

He stared at the grate, then turned to look at Christine. She was sitting bolt upright beside him, motionless, her face cold white against the dark hair that fell almost to her shoulders. Her teeth were clenched as she looked straight ahead. Angus flung an arm round her shoulder and held her tightly, saying nothing, waiting for her to speak.

'You thought a lot of Donnie,' he whispered at last. 'So did I.' Still she said nothing. At last Angus rose decisively and threw some peats into the grate.

'What will your mother say if she comes home and finds the fire out?' he said as lightly as he could. She remained silent, while tears made streaks down her face. He came and sat closer to her, took her in his arms.

'Christine,' he began hesitantly, 'I didn't mean to say anything to you this time. I wanted you to see first what it is like, with me being deaf. Maybe I will lose my hearing altogether. It could make things awkward.' He paused, with his characteristic frown of concentration, and looked for a response in Christine's eyes. But there was none. He pursed his lips as he only did when thought caused him peculiar stress.

'But anyway,' he went on, 'I'll tell you now what I meant to keep for later. I was going to ask you to marry me. Now say you'll marry me so I can hear you.'

'The wee parcel,' she forced between her lips, slowly and distinctly, 'it was a ring from Donnie.'

'But you're not wearing it,' was all Angus could find to say. Again there was silence.

'Were you going to marry Donnie?'

'He asked me.'

'I didn't hear.'

'I don't know.' She raised her voice to make certain he would hear this time. 'What's the use of asking me that now?' Angus gathered her more closely in his arms and kissed her wet cheeks.

'I'm sorry, Christine, I'm sorry. I should never have asked you to marry me just after hearing about Donnie. But I didn't know. We'll wait till later.' They were so close to each other that he easily heard what she said next.

'By then I'll have had Donnie's baby.'

Slowly Angus withdrew his arms and turned his gaze back to the fire. He glanced at the text hanging above it.

'To think,' he said, 'that I once nearly strangled a man for accusing you of that.' The effect of his remark on Christine was shattering. She flung herself at him, shouting, 'How did he know? Who was it?' But now it was Angus who kept her waiting as he stared at the flames in the grate, and far beyond them.

'He was a little English lad called Wright. But you need not worry. He is dead.' Suddenly Angus dropped his head between his hands and his shoulders became convulsed. 'It was dreadful,' he sobbed. The delayed reaction had been waiting all this time for such a catalyst.

'But you didn't kill him?' shouted Christine, a little hysterically. Angus turned to look at her, and at that moment there was a greater distance between them than the one that separated him from Tobruk. It was the gulf which everyone's personal experiences create between one another, that not even a lifetime of shared affection and understanding can bridge. Seeing it there, yawning between them, Angus found his feelings transformed. The war had injured both of them in different ways, but killed neither. If he could not explain what had happened to him, why should he expect her to account for what she had done? He took Christine in his arms again, and whistled the *Bonnie Lass of Bon Accord* to her. When he had finished, the frown of concentration returned to his brow.

'Have you told anyone?'

'Only Betsag. I gave her Donnie's ring to keep when it arrived.' Christine raised her voice as Angus strained to hear. 'People were asking questions about what was in the parcel.' Angus burst out laughing.

'What a long time we've taken to solve the mystery of the wee parcel,' he said. 'But the others haven't solved it. They think I sent it to you. It's funny, how much more you can make out sometimes, when you're deaf.' But while he was as high-spirited as he had been when he entered the house, or pretended to be, Christine remained as nervous as when he first set eyes on her. Her shoulders were hunched and she twisted her fingers in her lap.

'Was Tom there when you told Betsag?' Angus asked. His practical, extrovert character was reasserting itself.

'He was not in the room when I told Betsag, but I expect she has told him.' Christine was leaning towards him again confidingly, making sure he would understand.

'Tom is a far-out cousin of my own,' Angus reflected. 'He would always make a point of speaking to me. It is lucky we are not more nearly related, or they would be holding a *Comhairle*.' He looked at her enquiringly, to see whether she knew about the meeting of old people that was sometimes held when a Mackay wished to marry a Mackay, to discuss whether there was any weak strain that might endanger the union of people who were related to one another. She nodded.

'It is Betsag who is my mother's sister,' she reminded him. He rose with quick decision, put either hand on her shoulders and kissed her on the brow.

'Let me see you smile, lassie,' and she did. 'I'll be off now, but wait you till I'm back in the morning. I'll need to speak to your father.' He picked up his balaclava from the dresser and was out of the house almost before she could collect herself. She watched him stride down to the gate where his bicycle stood, a squat, purposeful figure. He gave her a single wave, started his machine and was gone into the darkness.

There was a drumming in his ears and his head ached painfully, yet he did not take the turning to his own home. He continued along the coast road, driving at a speed that nobody could have achieved who did not know every twist of it by heart. At the Point Inn he turned off up the gravel road that ran out of the house where Tom and Betsag lived. He bounced and lurched through the potholes, hardly slackening speed. The aurora was beginning to shine over the horizon to the north, moving fingers of pink and green, the Fir Chlis, as he came to the end of his hectic ride. Again the sound of his engine gave warning of his approach.

'Why, it's Angie Magnus,' Betsag called over her shoulder as she stood at the open door, waiting for him. 'Whenever did you get back? Come away in. You must be starved with the cold.'

162

'You'll have to shout, or I'll not hear you,' Angus told them as he shook hands with her, then Tom, then Tom's silent brother, Geordie.

'Oh aye, I heard that,' Tom said. 'Still, you're alive, and that's something to be thankful for. Do your ears still bother you much?' But he had not raised his voice sufficiently, so Angus fell back on his stock answer.

'I'm fine, thank you.' Geordie did not return to his seat by the fire but left the room.

'Why did he go?' asked Angus.

'He prefers his bed these cold nights,' Betsag told him. 'He has more sense than you.' Again Angus did not hear.

'I'm sorry I forgot to speak to him in Gaelic,' he said, as though this might be the reason why Geordie had left.

'Och no, he doesn't mind that,' Betsag said. 'But are you still going the Gaelic yourself, Angie?' She was closer to him now, and he was leaning towards her to hear.

'I was speaking it more in the army than ever I do at home,' he told her.

'Is that the truth you have?' she answered, opening her eyes wide in wonder. 'And me thinking no one could understand it south of Bonar Bridge!'

'When did you get home?' asked Tom, and added when Angus told him, 'it was good of you to come and see us so soon.' He walked out to the scullery and returned with a bottle and two glasses.

'The doctor told me I mustn't touch drink because of my ears,' said Angus.

'Man, isn't that just desperate?' exclaimed Tom, his eyes wide with sympathy. 'Are you sure just one would not do you good after your cold journey?' He had already poured a measure into one of the glasses.

'Yes, it would do me a lot of good,' said Angus taking it from him. '*Slainte mhath.*' And he swallowed it at a gulp.

'Now you sit in to the fire,' Betsag told him, and he took the chair that Geordie occupied as a rule.

'Donnie's dead,' he said, and as he looked at each of them in turn, he could tell that Betsag had told Tom. 'Seemingly he was in a plane and it crashed.'

'Where?' asked Tom.

'Somewhere out east according to the paper.' He saw Tom

163

and Betsag glance at one another in embarrassment.

'You'll take some hot soup to warm you, Angie,' said Betsag. 'There's plenty in the pot. I'm sorry about Donnie.'

'Thanks,' said Angus. 'I didn't go home for my tea. I was seeing Christine and then I came straight here. She told me she was pregnant and you are the only ones who know.' There was an immediate lightening of tension.

'You must have asked her to marry her before she would tell you that,' laughed Betsag, then added more seriously, 'Donnie asked her to marry him anyway.'

'Did she want to marry him, Betsag? Were they suited to each other, do you think?'

'Plenty people get married without finding out if they are suited to each other,' she answered him. 'Look at Tom and me for example.' Tom nodded in emphatic agreement, while Betsag went to put the pot on the fire.

'Anyway,' Angus told her, 'you're right. I did ask Christine to marry me. You must have the second sight.'

Then they began to talk about Donald, and Angus learned things about him that he had never known, nor Tom and Betsag either until Christine told her.

'I always thought Donnie was the luckiest person I ever knew,' said Angus. 'He had everything he could have wanted.'

'Christine said she thought he had everything except what he wanted,' Betsag replied.

'Well, what did he want?'

'Perhaps it was something he lost when he was sent away from here. Anyway it was something Christine could give back to him, more than just herself. I think maybe that was the secret of his hold over her. You know Christine.' Betsag went to ladle out the soup as though there was no more to be said and Angus sat at the table and ate hungrily.

'Christine talked about it so much when she was here,' Betsag added finally, 'but there is plenty we never know about others and now it is too late to find out any more.' Angus put down the spoon in his empty plate.

'Thank you, Betsag,' he said. 'Now I must be getting home. Mam will be wondering what has happened to me. If you will give me the ring, I will take it with me.'

Angus drove home recklessly through the darkness. The pain and the throbbing in his ears increased, confusing his thoughts and emotions, spurring him on. He missed a bend, his front wheel went into the drain beside the road, and he came off on the bank. But its heather made his landing a soft one. He picked himself up, man-handled his bike back on the road and continued more carefully. So he reached home safely, propped his bike against the stedding and re-entered his house. The pain in his head was intense as he pulled off his balaclava.

'Whatever's happened to you, lad?' asked his mother, looking first at the expression on his face, then at the stains of earth on his left trouser leg. Angus didn't hear her.

'You were right, Mam,' he said. 'I shouldn't have gone out on the bike. But it's just as well I did.' She came up to him and spoke slowly.

'Have you taken food?' she asked.

'I had soup with Betsag out at the Point.'

'You were out at the Point?' Jean asked in astonishment.

'I could drink a cup of tea though,' Angus went on, sinking wearily into his father's chair. 'Donnie's been killed. It's in the paper.' He took the two letters and the newspaper out of his inside pocket and put them on the shelf beside him. Jean raised the smoke-blackened kettle from its place beside the fire and hung it from the hook above.

'I hope he did not suffer,' she said. Then she waited for him to speak.

'Mam,' he asked, 'did you know about Donnie and Christine?'

'They were friendly,' she said into his ear. She was spooning tea out of the tin caddy on the mantelshelf into the enamel teapot.

'They were more than friendly. Christine is going to have a baby. Do you know when it would have happened?'

'When Donnie was up here before Christmas. It could only have been then.' Jean glanced towards the door of the closet bedroom. 'Christine was still a virgin then,' she said hastily.

'I am going to marry her anyway,' said Angus with an enquiring glance at his mother.'

'I'm glad,' she replied. 'She's a good girl and you are well suited to each other.'

'What about Donnie?' he asked. 'Was she suited to him?' She did not answer until she had poured water over the tea in the enamel pot and left it to infuse on the shelf beside the fire.

Then she came close to Angus and spoke carefully into his ear.

'I don't think Christine would have been happy with Donnie.' She had the frown of concentration that Angus had inherited as she searched in her mind for the right words. 'He was a lonely soul. It seemed as if he had nowhere to go.' She paused. 'He could not come – near – to people. I think Christine felt sorry for him.' She lifted the teapot and poured. And as Angus drank drank his cup of tea he told his mother everything that had occurred since he went to collect the mails.

'Your ears are bothering you,' she said finally. 'I can tell by your eyes.'

'I've had worse things to trouble me than my ears,' he replied and broke into his broad grin. 'Here, I'm forgetting the ring, and I haven't even seen it. Donnie sent it to Christine before he went away.' He fished for its little box in his pocket and they both examined the ring that Donald had chosen for her.

'Now I'll away to my bed,' said Angus. 'I'll need to speak to Bethel in the morning.'

'He will be the disappointed one,' said Jean, and they both laughed.

11

Angus awoke late the next morning, his headache still with him although it had diminished. The weather was warmer when he set out to walk to Bethel but he did not consider taking the bike. Apart from anything else, he had to conserve petrol. He had passed the manse before he stopped, then returned to it after a moment's thought. The Minister himself came to the door when he knocked.

It was a fortunate accident in the complicated situation that both Angus and Christine belonged to the Established Church. Long ago the congregation had called a Hebridean to this charge because a high proportion of them still wished to worship God in what they considered to be the true language of religion. The Minister held an afternoon service in Gaelic each Sabbath, although the morning one was now conducted in English. In a sense, those who believed that Gaelic was the more appropriate language in which to address God were proved right by their Minister. He could preach eloquently and clearly in Gaelic, whereas his English sermons tended to be a string of misquotations from the Bible and other sacred writings, strung together by word-association. For although he knew the English Bible almost by heart, he had never learned to think so well in English.

Angus greeted the Minister in Gaelic, and they continued to chat in that language after he had been invited into the manse. The Minister had once been heard to describe the speech of the Mackay country as *Gaidhlig uabhasach* – terrible Gaelic – and indeed it is a dialect unlike any other. But he had become accustomed to it, and perhaps regretted that there was a diminishing number of people with whom he could speak it. Angus reverted to English when it was time to come to the point.

'I wish to marry Christine Bethel, Mr MacDonald,' he said.

'I am pleased to hear that, Angus,' replied the Minister. 'She has God-fearing parents and she is a fine girl.' Angus found that although he had been able to hear the Minister when he spoke Gaelic, he could not understand what he said in English.

'I'm sorry, I'm not hearing you,' he apologized. 'I am on my way to speak to Christine's father, to ask him if I may marry her. I am hoping we can be married while I am here on leave. There will be time if the banns are called on the Sabbath coming.' He rose from his seat in the Minister's study.

'Mr Mackay will speak to me himself on the subject, no doubt,' said the Minister. 'If he is willing, I will do as you ask.' He walked back to the front door with Angus, and stood on its step. He was a little man, about the size of Wright, with the same directness that springs from goodness and simplicity. Indeed, if Wright had lived for another sixty years he might have turned into someone like this Minister, although the one came from a large English town, the other from a small Hebridean island.

As Angus walked on past the glebe fields, a skylark in full song sank slowly through the centre of a cluster of linnets until it reached the ground. He could not hear it, and as he stopped to watch the sight he became more acutely aware of his deprivation than at any time since he had returned home. He remained motionless while the skylark rose again, and saw the linnets adopt it as their leader and follow wherever it went. Only when they became a mere smudge in the sky did he resume his journey.

It was Christine's mother who came to the back door as Angus entered, a younger woman than her sister Betsag at the Point yet appearing older, with her lean careful face.

'Well, well, it's Angus,' she said, extending her hand and relaxing her stern expression slightly. 'We were very sorry to hear about you, but it's nice to see you back. Do come in.'

'I'm fine, thank you,' said Angus, using his stock phrase when he had not heard. 'How are you keeping yourselves?' He looked around, but Christine was nowhere to be seen, nor her father.

'Is Alec in?' he asked. 'I was hoping I would see him.'

'I'll call him.' And soon Christine's father appeared and they were exchanging civilities.

'You'll have to shout,' said Angus. 'I'm a bittie deaf and I'm not hearing you. I want to ask you about marrying Christine.'

'Marrying Christine?' echoed her father, and gave Angus his most imposing look. 'Come through.' He gestured Angus to the room at the other end of the house, and seated him between the harmonium and the silver-plated tray in its cabinet.

'I am grieved to learn that you have returned to us disabled,' he boomed in a pulpit voice that Angus could hear clearly, 'grieved indeed. But we must thank God that you have been spared at all. That is a great blessing.'

'I am not too disabled to marry,' Angus replied firmly, 'and if Christine will have me as I am I would like her to be my wife.'

'Christine has said nothing to us about wishing to marry you,' Bethel objected, 'and she is too young to marry anyone. Anyway, she has her career to think about.'

Angus rose from his seat, went to open the door and called out, 'Is Christine in the house?' Wherever she had been hiding previously, she was now in the kitchen, from where she walked through to the ben room.

'Good morning,' Angus said to her in a formal voice. 'Your father wishes to know if you would be willing to marry me.'

'Yes,' she replied, her eyes on the floor, 'I would like to marry you, Angus.' There was a long pause.

'Thank you, Christine,' said her father. 'You may leave us now.' As soon as the door was closed he embarked on a homily in which Angus gradually lost the thread of what he was saying, for it always cost him a great effort of concentration to listen and his mind was wandering to considerations of the next move. But he caught the term 'lusts of the flesh,' uttered with great emphasis, and agreed 'yes, yes' frankly. When he saw that Bethel had concluded his discourse, he gave his broad smile.

'I am grateful to you, Alec,' he said. 'I would not have wanted to marry Christine without your consent.' He paused, studying the look of astonishment on Bethel's face. 'I have four weeks' leave, all but a few days. That will give us time to marry before I go away.'

'That is impossible,' boomed Bethel. 'It would not be proper at all. It would not look decent.'

Angus had fought his way through too many minefields

since the previous evening to be defeated easily by his last obstacle. Bethel could see the tension in his fists, clenched in his lap, and hear it in the hardening of his voice.

'There is a war on, Alec,' he said. 'I have seen my friends killed before they have lived. None of us knows how long he will live, but Christine and I will share our lives together for as long as it pleases God to allow us. God, not you.'

'God, and his Minister of the Gospel,' Bethel replied loftily. 'Do you think the Minister would consent to anything of the sort?'

'He has given his consent already. I called to see Mr MacDonald on my way here, and he is only waiting for you to ask him to call the banns. They will have to be called the first time this coming Sabbath if we are to be married before my leave is up.'

The argument continued, but Angus had already won. Like so many bullies, Bethel crumbled before anyone who stood up to him firmly. Angus terminated the discussion by thanking Bethel and returning to the kitchen.

'Alec has given his consent,' he told Christine's mother. 'Will you mind if Christine comes back with me to see Mam? It would please her.' Christine was out in the scullery behind where she could hear his words, but she did not turn round. 'It will be a great honour for me to be a member of your family,' Angus said to her mother.

'Christine is not working today,' she replied, 'but she was to help me in the house.' She paused, then called into the scullery, 'off you go.' Angus did not hear, but he saw her dash to the peg where her coat hung, and then she was out of the house with him like an imprisoned bird whose cage door has been opened.

'How did you do it?' she shouted to him as soon as they were out of earshot of the house.

'For one thing, I pretended I did not hear when he was raising objections. Then he preached me a long sermon from his pulpit and I didn't listen except that I heard him warning me against the lusts of the flesh. Aye, there are advantages in being deaf.' He stopped in his tracks.

'But every blessing has its price. I shall never hear the lark again.' He put his head on her shoulder and whispered, 'You will have to be my lark.' Then they walked on for a while without speaking, through his silent world. They were passing beneath the rocks behind the bay when he put his hand in his pocket and took out the ring.

'You can put this on your finger now,' he told her. 'I would give you another, but I think Donnie would have liked you to wear this one.'

'You have been out to the Point?' she asked in astonishment, trying it on her finger. It fitted exactly.

'Yes, I think it's just right for you.'

When they reached Jack's house lower down the slope from Jean's, Angus suggested that they should call there on their way.

'It will give you a trial run,' he said. He ushered her into the untidy kitchen where two small children had pieces of a jigsaw puzzle scattered all over the floor. They were not trying to put the pieces together. They had them upside down, each marked with an M for Magnus, the marking for their sheep. Slowly, with proper concern for the topography of the floor, the little children were rounding up the jigsaw puzzle sheep. Hearing the visitors, Jack's wife came from upstairs, and in no time she was admiring the ring and asking the date of the wedding, and warning Christine solemnly to back out of it while she had the time.

'For heaven's sake,' said Angus, 'if you only knew the trouble I've had to make an honest woman of Christine, you would not even joke about it.'

At the door of Jean's house Christine held back, as though haunted by her memories.

'Don't be frightened,' Angus encouraged her. 'Just go you in.' He opened the door, giving her a slap on the buttocks. But he did not follow. He left Christine to speak with his mother alone while he wandered around at the back, his dog circling him all the time with its stomach close to the ground, its eyes expectant. At last he went in.

'I ought to take that lazy dog to the hill,' he said. 'Get outside with you,' he ordered, as it tried to trespass into the house after him. 'Are you feeling fit for a walk, Christine?'

'In that case you had better eat first,' suggested his mother, taking her assent for granted. She produced girdle scones, freshly baked, butter and crowdie of her own making, eggs which she placed in a pot over the fire to boil. 'The soup will not be ready in time,' she apologized, 'but you can take it when

171

you are back.'

They sat down at the table, and as soon as they were satisfied they strode away to the south, across the coast road and into the moors. It extended south for about thirty miles without a road or a habitation, in rising undulations of deer hair and sphagnum, dead grass and heather in which patches of crusted snow were dissolving. The hills beyond were still snow-capped, while the sea to the north was a smooth summer blue beyond the headland. The low sun left dark sockets in the uneven ground. Angus's dog would plunge ahead with great bounds, then select an eminence on which he could sit watching their approach. Finally they reached the area in which Angus expected to find his sheep, where the ewes returned with their lambs generation after generation, so that they recognized this territory as their own. He whistled to his dog to round them up and counted all thirty-two of them and found them in good condition.

'It should be a good year for the lambing anyway,' he said optimistically, although the weather might do anything in the interval.

'That's what I said to Donnie in my last letter,' Christine recalled.

'You were writing to him? You never wrote to me.'

'You never asked me to.' They set off towards home, turning their backs on the orange orb that was travelling south-west, not far above the white summits of the hills.

'Did you love Donnie very much?' Angus could not prevent himself from asking.

'I didn't really know him. He never told me anything about himself in his letters.'

'But surely you must have loved him when you went to bed with him.'

'I don't think you are ever going to forgive me for that,' said Christine, standing still. 'It will always come between us.'

'No it will not. Listen, Christine.' He took her hands in the thick paws that were the hallmark of the sons of Magnus. 'I am not proud to tell you this, but I think it may be helpful to you. I have had sex with other girls, when I had no love for them at all. It was just sex.'

'It wasn't like that with me and Donnie at all,' she expostulated.

172

'I know, I know.' He squeezed her hands so hard that she winced. 'That is not what I meant. I wanted you to know that I am not the one to forgive. Mind, I only did it twice. Some of the others were at it all the time.' She said nothing and they walked on.

'I didn't catch anything,' he assured her. 'We had blood tests, and they made us drop our trousers while they examined us. But you're a nurse, so you know all about that.'

'Yes,' said Christine.

'I expect you've seen so many of us that it's lost its novelty altogether.'

'You're to stop talking like this,' she shouted at him in sudden anger.

'No I am not,' he answered. 'If we are to know each other properly we must speak what is in our minds, even the bad thoughts, especially the bad thoughts. It is no use pretending we are better people than we are. I am going to be your husband, not Bethel's son-in-law.' He took her in his arms and kissed her, and a new lightness came into their tread after that.

They returned by way of the peat banks which lay in a basin about two miles south of the coast road. A rough cart track ran to them, on either side of which the exhausted peat grounds extended in a wilderness of waterlogged trenches. The pair walked along ridges between the new banks, past little stacks of peat that remained piled beside some of them. Their owners must have failed to get them home before the ground became impassable for horse and cart the previous year. Angus picked up one of the peats and broke it in two, inspecting how frost had taken the heart out of it. Wasted labour among the midges.

They reached the park of emerald green amongst the surrounding rocks and heather, in which stood the remains of a long-deserted township, houses built end-on to one another in a straight line. Their walls stood only to a few feet. Angus strode into the furthest of them and looked around him.

'This was where my great-grandfather came after he had been evicted from the strath,' he called. 'Until they were all evicted again and he reached the headland.'

'He couldn't go further.'

'Unless it was Canada where his brother went. But I'm glad he stayed here.' His dog was watching him from the high ground beyond. 'When I was at Tobruk I often thought of

173

these places and wondered would I ever see them again.' They wandered on.

'I've just thought of something,' said Angus. 'We'll need to tell Donnie's father and mother.'

'Would it be right to do that?' Christine pondered, but not so that he heard. She had grown used to shouting at him, but sometimes she forgot.

'Donnie was their only son, so this will be their only grandson.'

'If it's a boy.' Again he did not hear.

'It would not be fair to keep them in ignorance that they have a grandson. It would not be fair to the child either.' Christine came closer and raised her voice.

'But we can't prove it, and they might think it was their money we were after.'

'Don't be foolish,' Angus said, looking at her in astonishment. 'They're not like that, and they know we are not either. But it will be hard all the same.' The sun was sinking behind the hills of Assynt as this shadow fell upon them. They were nearing home when Angus turned to Christine with decision.

'There will be no time for a honeymoon before my leave is up, but I can go down to Inverness a day early and see the Hunters on my way.'

☆   ☆   ☆

Angus walked to the barracks on the outskirts of Inverness, obtained permission to spend the night there and left his kit.

It was Mrs Hunter who opened the door to him when he reached her home, and she did not recognize the squat figure in khaki and bonnet who stood before her.

'Good morning,' she said enquiringly.

'I'm afraid you will not remember me. I'm Angus.' He took off his bonnet nervously, as though this might help her to identify him. But the accents of the north coast, so different from those of the Moray Firth area, had already told her. She hesitated on the doorstep, timid and birdlike, her hands fluttering after they had shaken hands.

'Of course I remember you, Angus. It was just the surprise, and I haven't seen you in uniform before. In fact it's far too long since we saw you at all. How very good of you to come

174

now.' She talked on, quietly and fast, while she led Angus into the dining-room and closed the door behind them.

'I'm sorry to bring you in here,' she said, 'but I don't want my husband to see you. He's terribly upset about Donald. He's out visiting the hospital but if he comes back I would like to get him back to his corner without knowing you're here. You do understand, don't you. Norman's not very well, and the shock affected him badly.' She gestured to him to sit on one of the chairs at the dining-table and took another opposite to him.

Angus had heard nothing she had said. He gazed at the earnest, fragile face of Donald's mother, looking as encouraging as he could. He noticed the fine white hair, the skin like porcelain veined with tiny cracks, the suffering in her eyes.

'I'm sorry, Mrs Hunter, but I'm deaf,' he said, and came round the table to sit beside her. He took one of her hands.

'I want to tell you how sorry I am about Donnie,' he said. 'Everyone at home was asking me to send you their sympathy. I know how you and Captain Hunter must be feeling. We are all thinking of you.' Although his face was so close to hers, Mrs Hunter was looking at it distantly, as though it was a window through which she gazed into the past.

'Thank you, Angus. I appreciate what you have said very much, and so will Norman.' She glanced apprehensively at the window. 'How is your family at home, your mother and brothers?'

'I'm afraid I am still not hearing you. You will have to shout.' I was near a truck when it blew up at Tobruk and it has made me deaf. Some days I hear more than others, but just now I have a noise in my ears. Still, I am lucky to be alive.' He smiled at her encouragingly.

'I was asking after your mother,' she said with an effort, 'and your brothers.'

'Oh they're all fine, thank you. Neil was torpedoed but they rescued him.'

'And Christine? She was so kind to my husband when she was at the hospital here. We're both grateful.'

'I was married to Christine the day before yesterday.'

'What wonderful news! I'm so glad. Is she here with you? Why didn't you bring her with you?'

'I'm not quite sure what you said, Mrs Hunter, but there wasn't time for a honeymoon. My leave ends tomorrow and

I'm on my way south.' Mrs Hunter made the effort to raise her voice again.

'I wish I could ask you to stay with us here,' she apologized, glancing out through the window again.

'Thank you,' Angus lied, 'but I have to stay at the barracks.'

'Donnie would have been so pleased to know you and Christine are married,' Mrs Hunter reflected, then noticed Angus straining to hear with a puzzled expression. She raised her voice again. 'I think you and Christine were probably his closest friends. In fact, I sometimes wonder if you were his only friends.'

'He thought the world of Christine.' The frown of concentration came to Angus's face as he added slowly, 'I wonder whether he would have wanted to marry her himself, if he had lived.' He glanced at Mrs Hunter, and saw that Donald had not told his mother anything.

'I don't know,' she said. 'He was secretive. Perhaps that's why he was lonely.'

'I hope he had a happy life. I can remember him happy.'

'He was perfectly happy until we sent him away. You can remember him happy better than anyone although it is such a long time ago, because you were his closest companion then. We should never have sent him away so young. You must be sure to tell your mother how grateful we are that she always gave him a home to go back to.' Angus had been straining to catch her words, an ear close to her mouth.

'It was nothing,' he muttered. 'We were only sorry we did not see him more often.' He looked round the cold, elegant dining room, at the polished mahogany table so unlike the little one in his own warm kitchen, 'but he had a fine home here.'

'He hardly looked on this place as his home,' said Mrs Hunter. 'It was just somewhere to spend holidays and visit his parents. If we had not moved from the north coast it might have been different.'

'But Donnie couldn't have spent all his life on the north coast. It's different for us. I have the croft and Christine's a nurse.'

'Yes I know. But we gave him that world at the start of his life and then took it away from him, and he never found another to replace it.' She gazed past him and dropped her voice so that Angus could no longer hear her. 'I wonder

176

whether he was fond of Christine because she was the symbol of his lost childhood world.' Angus interrupted her train of thought.

'Life is strange,' he said. 'When there are so many people who must have envied Donnie, I think he might have exchanged Hunter and Jones's Brewery for my croft.' He rose from the table and picked up his bonnet that had been lying on it. 'I must be going now, Mrs Hunter. But I want you to know that we never forget old friends, and where Donnie wanted to be he will be remembered always. It will be as though he is still there amongst us.'

Although he had never kissed his own mother, he flung his arms round Mrs Hunter's fragile shoulders and kissed her. Then he strode out of the house in which Donald had concealed from his mother that he had asked Christine to marry him. If Donald had not wanted this place for his home, it should not be his child's either.

Angus had made a number of difficult decisions that would affect the future of the living for ever. Now he had made another for somebody not yet born, and as he stood waiting by the roadside to hitch-hike back to Inverness he sagged with a weariness that was emotional rather than physical. He did not ask to be put down at the barracks but rode on into the town, where the pubs had opened. There he disobeyed the doctor's orders and drank himself into a state close to oblivion. His companions steered him back to the barracks and saw him safely to his train in the morning.

After he had returned to his unit, his case was resolved. It was noted that he had not been a conscript, but a volunteer from the reserved occupation of agriculture. So instead of spending the remainder of the war in non-combatant duties he received an immediate discharge, and was able to return home soon for his delayed honeymoon.

They spent it in London, because Angus arrived home to learn that he had received a gallantry award. Donald had promised Christine that he would take her to the home of Sir William and Lady Jones there. Instead she went with Angus to Buckingham Palace.

12

Angus was on his way to the potato rig when his boys scampered towards him. They were on their own more, now that their mother had taken up district nursing again. Christine had been doubtful whether she ought to go out to work before they were older, but when the local vacancy occurred Angus advised her to put in for it. She travelled about in a little black Ford Popular car.

'Can we go down to the port, Dad?' called the elder of the two boys.

'If you're back by dinner time. Now listen, Donnie. If you go out on the rocks, you're to look for a steep wall that has a funny mark in it.' He crooked one of his arms. 'It's bent like this, but it's much bigger and it's dark. You would think it's a huge iron spring buried in the rock. You can't miss it if you watch out, and you're not to go beyond it, or you may be cut off by the tide. When you reach it, you come straight back to your dinner, the two of you.'

Angus could never tell when Christine would return from her visits, but it didn't matter because Jean was there to prepare the food. But for her, Christine would probably not have agreed to return to nursing. Of all her nine grandchildren, Jean watched over Donald with the most careful attention.

'You leave him to me,' she said once when Christine expressed some worry concerning him.

Jean slept in the downstairs closet, so that she enjoyed a measure of privacy with the run of the house after the family had retired upstairs to bed. Soon she would also be enjoying greater comfort because piped water and electricity were to be brought to the district, and Angus was preparing to add a bathroom at the back of the house, beside her bedroom.

It was holiday time, hitherto marred by a spell of rain, as so often occurred in August. The boys ran off with all the more glee in the sunshine, after being confined by the wet weather. But when they reached the top of the zigzag path that ran down to the port, the younger of them drew back. He was over a year younger than his brother, not quite seven.

'I'll never get down there, Donnie,' he said. 'It's too steep.' The embankments of the track were crumbling fast by now, falling away into loose scree.

As the boys stood perched above it, Neil's boat came into sight, returning from the other side of the headland where he had thrown his lobster creels beyond the rocks.

'You stay here, Angie. I'll go down and see Neil and then come back. I won't be long and you can call if you want me.' He went slithering down the path and stood on the shingle, waiting for Neil to bring his boat in to the concrete jetty that jutted from the right side of the cove. Only a few yards of water separated them in the sudden silence when Neil switched off his engine.

'You never took me to the island, Neil,' Donald called. Neil straightened himself amongst the disorderly tackle in his boat, stared across at him, and scratched his ear.

'I offered to take you once,' he shouted back, 'even though the boat was too full already, but you wouldn't come.' Donald stared back, looking even more puzzled than Neil.

'You did not,' he insisted. 'You never asked me, or I would have come.'

'Ah well,' Neil conceded, 'perhaps it was somebody else. You look awful like someone I knew. But I'll take you to the island soon. That's a promise.' They both looked up as the tiny figure of young Angus gesticulated and called to them from the top of the cliff. The basin which formed the cove possessed the acoustics of an amphitheatre.

'It's all right, Angie. I'm just coming up,' his brother called.

It was a slow climb up that ruined path, and as young Angus sat watching him his back was turned to his home beyond the football field. So he did not notice the woman with white hair who came to its front door, so seldom used, and knocked. But Jean had seen her through a window, walking up the slope, and was already at the door to greet her.

'Why, it's Mrs Hunter. I'm very pleased to see you. Come

away in.'

'I do hope I'm not disturbing you, Mrs Mackay,' said Mrs Hunter, hesitating diffidently on the doorstep. 'I've always wanted to come and see you, to thank you for your kindness to Donald, but it wasn't easy to get away while my husband was living. He was an invalid, you know.'

'Yes, I was sorry to hear of your bereavement. Come through. Have you been up here long?'

'No, I came to the hotel last night. I will only stay a day or two.'

They had reached the kitchen, where a new armchair had replaced the one in which Magnus had sat and there was a bright new linoleum floor covering. But the old open fireplace with its brass rail above still survived.

'I'm sorry not to take you to the room,' Jean said, inviting her guest with a gesture to take the armchair while she seated herself on the couch opposite. 'The boys will be back for their dinner soon and Christine is out at the nursing.' The two women chatted of family matters and then of old times, while Jean rose occasionally to continue her preparations for the meal.

There was a sound of approaching children, both talking at once, then they stampeded in through the back door and appeared at the entrance to the kitchen. Instantly they became silent and bashful. They were not accustomed to strangers, particularly ones who appeared without notice in their home.

'Go and wash your hands,' Jean told them. 'Then you can come and meet Mrs Hunter.' They slunk back into the scullery, where they could be heard whispering to each other over the sink while they took a most unusual length of time to wash.

'Hurry up, the two of you,' called Jean. 'Your soup is on the table.' They returned to shake hands with Mrs Hunter, then slid on to their seats and began to eat with concentration. But their spirits were not repressible for long, and it was young Angus who exploded first.

'Neilie came back to the port in his boat,' he began to narrate in a rush, 'and Donnie told him he had not kept his promise to take him to the island and Neilie said I did so but you would not come and Donnie said you did not and then Neilie said if it was not Donnie it was another boy who looked like him.'

'Shut your mouth, Angie,' Donnie hissed at him, trying to kick him under the table.

'He did. I heard him,' young Angus insisted.

'You behave yourselves,' Jean scolded them, 'or you will go without your dinner. You should be ashamed of yourself, Donnie, kicking Angie like that. What will Mrs Hunter think?'

Donnie turned to look at Mrs Hunter from behind his spoon, and saw her gaze fixed on him. Hastily he put another potato in his soup and began to eat.

'How old are you, Donnie?' she asked him.

'Eight.'

'And when is your birthday?' He told her.

'Mine is next month and then I will be seven,' added Angus, evidently considering this to be of equal interest.

But his grandmother deflected Mrs Hunter from her interest in birthdays by talking to her about something quite different. No further attention was paid to the children as they finished their meal, although Donald had an impression that Mrs Hunter kept looking at him. So he was even more eager than usual to run out of the house as soon as he had finished.

'Thank you, Gran,' he called, running through the scullery.

'Come back, Donnie,' she ordered. 'You have not said goodbye to Mrs Hunter. That is not polite.' Smugly, young Angus went up to Mrs Hunter first and shook hands with her.

'Goodbye,' he said with the broad grin she had seen before. Donald trailed back and stood before her, a troubled expression on his face. It was she who held out her hand to him.

'Goodbye, Donnie,' she said. 'I hope I shall see you again.' He took her hand but could find nothing to say before running out into his familiar world.

'You may think it wrong that we didn't tell you, Mrs Hunter,' Jean said as soon as the children were gone. 'But we thought it would be best for the child.'

'Why?'

'Because you might have wanted to share him with us, and then he would have been tossed back and fore between two different worlds. It would not have been good for him.'

'I know,' Mrs Hunter agreed. She stared abstractedly at the brass rail, then added as though talking to herself, 'it's what happened to his father.'

181

'I don't want to hurt your feelings,' Jean continued, 'but there is something I must tell you because it would be fair to Donnie. When Angie came to see you after Donnie was killed, he thought you must know, then he discovered you did not.' Jean was speaking very slowly, twisting her fingers in her lap as she searched for the words that would give least pain. 'Donnie did ask Christine to marry him, in fact he sent her a ring. Everyone thinks it was Angie gave it to her, but it was Donnie who sent it before he went abroad. I'm sorry he did not tell you himself.'

Mrs Hunter rose abruptly, one hand on her chest. Jean eyed her anxiously.

'Will you not stay and eat with us? Angie will be back soon and perhaps Christine as well.' But Mrs Hunter simply stood there, swaying slightly and looking vaguely about her as though uncertain whether to escape by the front door or the back. She trailed to the scullery entrance, then turned.

'Not now, thank you,' she whispered, then added pitifully, 'but you will let me come anther time? I would like to see little Donnie again. I have no one else.'

'Of course. Come tomorrow at about this time and we will all be here.' She stopped, once again choosing her words carefully. 'But you will not try to take Donnie away, will you? We have not so much to offer him as you have, but he is happy here.'

'No no,' Mrs Hunter promised.

'Perhaps you would like us to tell him when he is older,' Jean suggested, 'when he has had time to know you better. Please come tomorrow. It will be a start.'

Mrs Hunter set off down the path that led to the sands. As she passed the football field she saw the two boys kicking a ball between one of its renovated goalposts. She turned to wave, a timid, fluttery gesture. Donnie noticed it as he was about to kick the ball, and watched her out of the corner of his eye as he positioned himself with greater care. The ball flew straight between the posts and into the reeds, where Angus ran to retrieve it. Meanwhile Donnie turned to Mrs Hunter with a smile of triumph. His expression was open and strangely intimate.

Mrs Hunter gazed at him with wide eyes as one of her hands clutched again at her chest and her mouth opened, though she said nothing. Then she collapsed on the cropped grass of that gentle slope. Donnie came running over to her. He shook her gently.

'Wake up, Mrs Hunter,' he pleaded. 'Wake up.'

But Mrs Hunter did not wake up. The last strand had snapped that bound him to the past.